"Throughout, Malzberg's prose—perhaps the finest in science fiction—weaves a state of lyric darkness. . . This promises to be the science fiction novel of the year."

—*The Boston Phoenix*

THE
CROSS
OF
FIRE

BARRY N. MALZBERG

SF
ace books
A Division of Charter Communications Inc.
A GROSSET & DUNLAP COMPANY
51 Madison Avenue
New York, New York 10010

THE CROSS OF FIRE
Copyright © 1982 by Barry N. Malzberg

An earlier version of this novel, in much shorter form, appeared in THEIR IMMORTAL HEARTS and is copyright
© 1980 by West Coast Poetry Review.

An ACE Book

First Ace printing: May 1982
Published Simultaneously in Canada
2 4 6 8 0 9 7 5 3 1
Manufactured in the United States of America

THE CROSS OF FIRE

For Margaret Susan Allison

Depersonalization takes him over once again and as usual he does not quite feel like himself. This is for the best: the man as he is known could hardly manage these embarrassing circumstances. Adaptability, that is the key. Swim the fast waters. There is no other way that he, let alone I, could get through.

"Pardonnez tout ils," he says, feeling himself twirling upon the crucifix in the absent Roman breezes, a sensation not unlike flight. "Mais ils ne comprendre pas que ils fait."

Oh my, oh my, is that awful! He wishes that he could do better than that. Still, there is no one around, strictly speaking, to criticize and besides he is merely following impulse which is the purpose of the program. I can do what I want, he tells himself. "Ah pere this is a bitch," he mutters.

The thief to his left, an utterly untrustworthy type, murmurs curses, and the man, losing patience with his companions who certainly *look* culpable, guiltiest pair he ever met, stares down. Casting his glance he thinks he can see the onlookers, not so many as one would hope, far less than the Gospels would indicate but certainly enough (fair is fair and simple Mark had made an effort to get it right) to cast lots over his vestments. They should be starting that stuff just about now.

Oh, well. This too shall pass. He considers the sky, noting with interest that the formation of clouds against the dazzling sunlight must yield the aspect of stigmata. For everything, a natural explanation. It is a rational world back here after all, if a little on the monolithic side.

"I wonder how long this is going to go on," he says. Just making conversation while the blood congeals. "It does seem to be taking a long time."

"Long time?" the thief on the left says. "Until we die, that's how long, chief, and not an instant sooner. It's easier," the thief adds confidentially, "if you breathe in tight little gasps. Less pain. You're kind of grabbing for the air."

"Am I? Really?"

"What you got to try to do is not reach so deeply inside yourself," the thief says helpfully. "Pant a little; you get more shallow than going far inside. There's less pain, too."

"I'll have to try that."

"It's a matter of experience," the thief says mysteriously. "You go through these things, you learn."

"Leave him alone," the other thief says. "Don't talk to him. Why give advice? Do you think that

2

he'd give *you* any help? The filthy buggers nailed you up here in the first place; that's how much caring there is."

"Just trying to help a mate on the stations, that's all."

"Help *yourself,*" the second thief grumbles. "That's the only possibility."

"Didn't get you no different place, chief?" the first thief says almost cheerfully. "Did it now?"

"No it didn't," I say. "We've all wound up in exactly the same place and so much for human circumstance."

"Stuff it chief."

"Where?" I say but there is no answer. So much for relationships. It is impossible to deal with these people. The texts imbue them through sentimental focus with what I might call pathos but, truly, they are swine. I can grasp Pilate's dilemma.

Thinking of Pilate as my blood rots leads me into another channel, the question of choices as they cross with circumstance, motive with fate but before I can truly consider these interesting metaphysical issues, pain of new dimension slashes and there I am, there I am, suspended from the great cross groaning, all the syllables of thought trapped within.

"Ah," I murmur, "ah," he murmurs. "Ah, monsieurs, c'est le plus," but it is not to be sure *le plus* at all. There are always further levels of potential descent.

Indeed there are and it goes on, in fact, for an unsatisfactorily extended and quite spiritually laden period of time. The lot casting goes quickly and there is little to divert on the hillside; one can only take so much of that silly woman's cries before all emotional impact is lost. It becomes a long and screaming difficulty, a passage broken only by the careless deaths of the thieves who surrender in babble and finally, not an instant too soon, the man's brain bursts . . . but there is time, crucifixion being what it is, for further slow dimunition. Lessened color; black and grey. If there is one thing to be said about the process it is this: it is exceeding generous. One will be spared nothing.

Of course I had pointed out that I did not want to be spared anything. "Give me Jesus," I had asked and cooperating in their patient way they had given me Jesus. There is neither irony nor restraint to the process and this is exactly the way that it should be.

The thief's instructions on how to breathe were a particularly good touch: I can appreciate fine work on every level. I am not unaware of the value of fine work.

"Depersonalization, the tendency to think of or refer to oneself in the third person, is one of the characteristics of schizophrenia, you know," he said to me. "It is an ancient and mysterious disease about which we have not been able to do as much as we had hoped."

"Is that so?" I said. "Is that so?" he said. "What is it exactly?" the man asked.

"The slow or rapid shattering of the psyche, the disintegration of the personality. Once considered to be functional in origin but now suspected to have an organic base, to be caused by a circulatory or cellular imbalance. Of course," the advisor said, "this is completely off the record. It is considered quite risky to discuss symptoms or diagnosis with the subject."

"I appreciate your doing that."

"Not to mention. Just keep it in confidence."

"Oh I will," I said, "I won't tell anyone."

"I'll deny everything if you say that I've been sharing confidential information with you."

"I am a man of honor," he said. "I am not only a voyager but a conservative."

Alive, alive to the tenor of the strange and difficult times, I found myself moved to consider the question of religious knowledge as it may blur into fanaticism. Hard choices have to be made even in pursuit of self-indulgence. Both were dangerous to the technocratic state of 2219 of course, but of the two religion was considered the more risky because fanaticism could well be turned to the advantage of institutions. (The state did not know, as I did, that the two were often indistinguishable.) Sexuality was another pursuit possibly dangerous to the state but it held no interest for me; the general Privacy and Social Taboo acts of the previous century had been taken very seriously by my subdivision and I inherited neither genetic nor socially-derived interest in sex for its own non-procreative sake.

Religion interested me more than fanaticism for a permanent program but fanaticism was not without its temptations. "Religion, after all, imposes a certain rigor," I was instructed. "There is some kind of rationalizing force and also the need to learn a good deal of material. Then too there is the reliance upon another, so to speak higher, power. One cannot ultimately fulfill narcissistic tendencies. On the other hand fanaticism dwells wholly within the poles of self. You can destroy the systems, find immortality, lead a crushing revolt, discover immortality within the crevices. It is not to be neglected; it is also purgative and satisfying and removes much of that indecision and social alienation of which you have complained. No fanatic is truly lonely. He has learned to bear his isolation in grandeur."

"I think I'd rather have the religious program," I say after having considered all of this. "The lives of the prophets, the question of the validity of the text, matters of the passion attract me."

"You will find," they pointed out, "that much of the religious experience is misinterpreted. It leads only to increasing doubt for many and most of the religious figures of history were severely maladjusted. You would be surprised how many were psychotics whose madness was retrospectively falsified by others for their own purpose."

"Still," I said, "there are levels of feeling worth investigating. Levels of belief."

"That of course is your decision," they said, relenting. Pressed on the point they will always relent; this is how they maintain their power. Under the revised acts of 2202 severely liberalizing board procedures there have been many improvements of this illusory sort. "If you wish to pursue religion we will do nothing at all to stop you. It is your inheritance and our decree. We can only warn that there is apt to be disappointment."

"Disappointment!" I screamed, allowing affect to bloom perilously forth. "I am not interested in disappointment. This is of no concern to me whatsoever; what interests me is the *truth*. After all and was it not said that it is the truth which shall make ye free?"

"Not in this lifetime," they say, "you will find that it is very much different here," and sadly, sadly they cut me off and sent me on my way with a proper program, a schedule of appointments with the sinister technicians, the necessary literature to explain the effect that all of this would have upon my personal landscape: inevitable changes, the rules of dysfunction, little instances of psychotic break, but all of it to be contained within the larger pattern. By the time I exit the transverse I have used up the literature and so I dispose of it, tearing it into wide strips, throwing strips into the empty, sparkling air above the passage lanes, watching them catch the little filters of light for the moment before they flutter soundless to the metallic, glittering earth of this most unspeakable yet interesting time.

"I'm sorry," Pilate said. His eyes did indeed seem reflective. "I offered them a choice; I would have been willing to accept their judgement. Barabbas is a fine fellow, very popular nowadays; perhaps I should have forced the issue—"

"It's all right," I say, "I don't mind. Let's get on with it."

"You don't understand," Pilate says. "Crucifixion is an extremely painful process; you would have to have undergone it to know of what I am speaking, but it is not to be taken lightly. You'll see what I mean." His eyes become vague, he clutches his robes. "Perhaps we could have a recount," he says, "another ballot or failing that I could allow you to slip out the side, say that the prisoner escaped, there's precedent for that and besides—" His voice mumbles off. "No," he says, "it can't possibly work. There's got to be a crucifixion; I just wish that there were some way not to go through with it."

"I am ready," I say, "let it be done."

"You're saying that now," Pilate shrugs, "but later on you'll be thinking differently. Oh well," he says after a pause, "there really is no free will, we have to come to understand that and I'm not prepared to separate you from what you take to be your destiny." He walks to an alcove, gestures. "You'll just be on your way, then."

"I'm really grateful for the opportunity that you're giving me," I say, "you don't think so but it's true. You don't know how much you're helping."

"One of the characteristics of schizophrenia," Pilate points out quietly, "is disassociation reaction, a separation from the physical consequences of one's acts. One regards oneself as insensate machinery, not capable of feeling."

The soldiers enter.

"Let's go," I say boldly.

Pilate sighs and turns away.

* * *

I find myself at an earlier point of the process the Grand Lubavitcher Rabbi of Bruck Linn, administering counsel to all who would seek it. The Lubavitcher Sect of the Judaic religion was, I understand, a twenty- or twenty-first reconstitution of the older, stricter European forms which were composed of refugees who fled to Bruck Linn in the wake of one of the numerous purges of that time. Now defunct, the Judaicists are, as I understand, a sect characterized by a long history of ritual persecution from which they or at least the surviving remnants flourished but then again the persecution might have been the most important part of the ritual. At this remove in time, it is hard to tell. The hypnotics, as the literature and procedures have made utterly clear, work upon personal projections and do not claim historical accuracy as historical accuracy exists. The times being what they are. The times are not oriented toward history.

It is, in any case, interesting to be the Lubavitcher Rabbi in Bruck Linn; regardless of the origins of the sect or its reality there is a certain power in it. I can respect power even as I administer it. In frock coat and heavy beard I sit behind a desk in cramped quarters surrounded by murmuring advisors and render judgements one by one upon members of the congregation as they appear before me. Penalty for compelled intercourse during an unclean period is three months of abstention. I mete that out despite explanations that the young bride had pleaded for comfort. The

Book of Daniel no matter how perused does *not* signal the resumption of Holocaust within the coming month; the congregant is sent away relieved. Two rabbis appear with a Talmudic dispute: one says that Zephaniah meant that merely all pagans, not all things were to be consumed utterly off the face of the Earth but the other says that the edict of Zephaniah was literal and that one cannot subdivide "pagans" from "all things". I return to the text for clarification, remind them that Zephaniah no less than Second Isaiah or the sullen Ecclesiastes spoke perversely and advise that the literal interpretation would have made this conference unecessary and therefore metaphor must apply. My advisors nod in approval. There are gasps of wonder and admiration. Bemused the two rabbis leave, hand in hand. A woman asks for a ruling on *mikvah* for a pre-menstrual daughter who is nonetheless fifteen and on this I wisely reserve decision. A conservative rabbi from Yawk comes to give humble request that I give a statement to his congregation for one of the minor festivals and this I decline pointing out that for the Lubavitcher fallen members of the Judaicists are more reprehensible than those who have never arrived. Once again my advisors applaud. There is a momentary break in the consultations and I am left to pace the study alone while advisors and questioners withdraw to give me more time for contemplation.

It is interesting to be the Lubavitcher, although somewhat puzzling. One of the elements of which I was not aware was that in addition to the grander passions, the greater persona, I would also find myself enacting a number of smaller roles, the busy worker ants of the religious life as it were and it was pointed out to me that I must observe them no less rigorously. Faith is discipline; passion is formed against stone.

So I am accepting but the absence of emotion in the persona of the Lubavitcher Rabbi is puzzling. The questions of Talmudic interpretation are arid: what do they have to do with the thrashings of Calvary? Nevertheless, the indoctrinative techniques have done their job; I am able to make my way through these roles even as the others on the basis of encoded knowledge and although the superficialities I babble seem meaningless to me, they seem to please those who surround. I adjust my cuffs with grandeur; Bruck Linn may not be all of the glistening spaces of Rome but it is not an inconsiderable part of history and within it I seem to wield a great deal of power. (This was certainly not true in Rome.)

"Rabbi," an advisor says, opening the door, "I hesitate to interrupt your musings."

I look up at him, an uneasy young chassid with an open, wistful face. "Then why interrupt them at all?"

"We have a crisis."

"Life is a crisis."

"This is a particular crisis and your intervention is needed at this time."

"It is dangerous to interrupt me at brooding," I say. A squall of panic whisks across the chassid's face. "Anything might happen," I say. "Or fail to happen."

"We *respect* your meditations, Rabbi. It is wrong to impose, I am shamed to do so, I argued against it but they insisted, they said that one must go to talk to him—"

Some edge of agony within his voice, the broken aspect of his face touches me even as he stumbles against the door. "This is not necessary," I say, standing. "Very well then, what is it?"

"We will protect, Rabbi," he says, "we will respect, we will fructify and relate and pray," and now I am really concerned; from large hat to enormous pointed shoe he is trembling. I push past him into the dense and smoky air of the vestibule where congregants, advisors, women and children have gathered. As they see me their faces one by one register intent and then they are screaming, their voices inchoate but massed. *Save us, Rabbi,* they are saying, *save us* and I do not know what is going on here, an awkward position for a Talmudic judge to be sure but I simply do not know; I push my way through the clinging throng pushing them aside, oh my God, Rabbi, they are saying, oh my God, and I thrust by them to the outer doors, stare down the street and see the massed armaments, see the troops eight abreast moving in great columns toward the building, behind them the terrible engines of the night and in the sky, sound. The Holocaust, Rabbi, someone says, the Holocaust has come, they will kill us and I feel disbelief. What is going on? How can this be happening? There was no purge in Bruck Linn to the best of my recollection; there have never been any great purges on this part of the continent. Nevertheless, here they are and behind me I can hear the children screaming. It is all that I can do to spread my arms and facing the massed congregants and advisors say, "Be calm, this is not happening. It is an aspect of the imagination, some misdirection of the machinery. It is a case of historical anachronism and even at this moment it is being corrected."

Surely it must be that, some flaws in the fabric of my own perception being fed through the machines, creating history out of context and yet the thunder and smell of the armies is great in the air and I realize that they are heading directly toward this place, that they have been coming toward it all this time and that there is nothing I can do to stop them.

"Be calm, be calm," I cry, "you are imagining this, indeed you are all imagining," but the words do not help, and as I look at the people, as they look at me, as the sounds of Holocaust overwhelm, I seem to fall through the situation, leaving them to a worse fate . . . or perhaps it is a better and it is only I who have exited, leaving the rest, these fragments of my imagination, to shore themselves against their ruins and not a moment not a moment not a moment too soon.

"Events may occur out of sequence, strange intrusions may be found in the replications, the texts may not be accurately reproduced," they had pointed out to me. "We are dealing not with objective truth, all of this is opinion anyway, but with your *perceptions* of the truth and if they are skewed or faulty so will the events be. We can only order your mind and project, we cannot really structure it anew; we cannot put in what is not there and it is your interior which will be re-enacted over and again."

"No problem," I said, somewhat smugly I admit. "I have more knowledge of these texts than you do, more than anyone in these desolate times. Anachronisms will be kept to a minimum."

"Nonetheless you must be alerted. Events as portrayed may not be as you had suspected; it is your unconscious which will be rendering the images and the unconscious is stupider than you might think."

"Administrators, clerks, third-level servants of the distant and gleaming engines," I said, "don't threaten me; simply be technicians and make the proper adjustments."

So, efficiently and without further counsel, they did.

Outside of the machines, life proceeds as always. The hypnotics and the project must be served but there are commitments otherwise: to eat, sleep, participate in the slight but always bizarre social activities of the complex; even, on occasion, to copulate which I accomplish with method to the madness. The construction, I have been counselled, is only a portion of my life; responsibilities do not cease on its account. I maintain my cubicle, convey the usual depositions from level to level, busy myself in the perpetuation of microcosm. Only at odd times do I find myself thinking of the nature of the hypnotic experiences and then I try to push the recollections away. They are extremely painful and this subtext, as it were, is difficult to integrate into the wider arch of my life. In due course I am assured that fusion will be made but in the meantime it cannot be hastened.

"You have changed, Harold," Edna says to me. Edna is my current companion. She is not named Edna nor I Harold but these are the names assigned for contemporary interaction and Harold is as good as any; it is a name by which I would as soon be known. Harold in Galilee. And I have spoken his name and it is Harold. She leans toward me confidentially. "You are not the same person that you were."

"That is a common illusion provided by the treatments," I say. "I am exactly the same person. Nothing is any different than it was."

"Yes it is," she murmurs. "You have become very withdrawn and distracted."

She is an attractive woman, this Edna, and there are times during our more or less mechanical transactions when I have felt real surges of feeling but they have only been incidental to the main purpose. In truth I am incapable of feeling for anyone but myself; I found this out a long time ago. It was a difficult insight but enriching. "I don't think that's so," I say to her. "The process doesn't affect the outer life, certainly not at the beginning. They were very clear on this."

She puts an intense hand against mine. "What are they doing to you? Tell me the truth."

"Nothing," I say quite truthfully. "It is merely what they are permitting me to do to myself, bringing out of me. They are merely providing the equipment. Everything that is done I am doing myself, this is the principle of the treatment. Otherwise, for instance, there would be no anachronisms."

"You are deluded," she says. She loops an arm around me, drags me into stinging but pleasurable embrace. Forehead to forehead we lay nestled amidst the bedclothes; I feel the tentative stroke of fingers. "Now," she says, moving her hand against me. "Do it now. You'll like it."

I shrink at her embrace. "No, it's impossible."

"Why?"

"During the treatments it can't be done. The sympathetic nervous system has been altered, there are neurological changes—"

"Nonsense," Edna says. "You're avoiding me, that's all. You're avoiding yourself. The treatments are anaesthetic, don't you see that? They are forcing you to avoid the terms of your life and you cannot do that." Her grasp becomes insistent, moves toward the lip of pain. "Come on," she says. Insistent woman. Against purpose, I feel a slow gathering.

"No," I mutter against her cheekbone, "it can't be done and I refuse."

"Fool."

"The chemicals. I'm awash in them; I'm in a sustained dose all the time. I would upset all of the balances, I might be set back by months—"

"You understand nothing."

"I'm following instructions."

"Nothing," she says but in an inversion of mood

turns from me, draws up her knees. "Have it as you will? Do you want me to leave you alone?"

"Of course not. I want you here with me. Why would I want you to go?"

"Of course not; of course not. You are so accommodating. Do you want me to entertain you? Talk about the scriptures, go over the Gospels point by point? Drag out those hideous things and begin to read the psalms again?"

"That would be very nice," I say. "I'd like that if you wouldn't mind; it would be helpful."

"You've changed completely. You're not the same at all; you're not acting rationally. These treatments have rendered you cataleptic. Harold, I had hopes for you, I want you to know that; I thought there were elements of genuine perception, real thought. How was I to think that all of the time you were escaping into me you really wanted to escape into your fantasies?"

"What did you expect me to do?" I say casually. "Overthrow the mentors? Change the circumstance?"

She shrugs. "Why not? That would be something interesting and different to keep us occupied."

"I'd rather overthrow myself."

"You know, Harold," she says, and there is clear, steady light of implication in her eye, "it's not impossible for me to like you; we could really come to understand one another, work together to deal with this crazy situation but there is this one overwhelming problem."

"I know what it is."

"You are a fool, Harold."

"I've heard that before."

"Don't deprive me of the satisfaction," she says, "it's all that I'm going to have left."

"Well," I say, "well, then, in these perilous and difficult times, this madly technocratic age of 2219 I should say when we have so become merely the engines of our institutions, where any search for individuality must be accomplished by moving within rather than without, taking all of this into consideration and with one thing being like every other thing in this homogeneous world, tell me Edna, aren't we all? Aren't every one of us?"

"Not like you," she says, "oh Harold, even in these perilous and difficult times, not like you at all."

Limping from the effects of an old sprain incurred during the competitions, I go to see the Confessor. Edna has troubled me, now and then she is capable of reaching the emotional center. "*Is* it the sin of pride?" I say when I have given the background, "am I overreaching?"

"Common in these times," the old man says. He turns a page, runs a finger until he finds the procedural response. "It is quite acceptable to trace the roots of one's history. Thousands do it, millions more would if they had your economic opportunity. I wouldn't feel guilt about it."

"My companion is trying to make me feel that way."

"Unless you need to feel guilt. That is a different issue of course. Do you seek humiliation?"

"Certainly not. The program seeks transcendence."

"Then don't worry about it," the Confessor says. He stares at me until I realize that he has nothing more to say. Awkwardly, I stand. "I appreciate your time," I say.

"Think nothing of it. Whatever penance you seek will be paid in the machines," the Confessor says, "and that is a certainty." He seems to wink at me; his other eye, enormous, swims golden in his head. "My pleasure, son," he says.

I pay him the standard fee and leave. In the hall it occurs to me that the program offers nothing but humiliation for a very difficult and still-disputed transcendence and I turn back to discuss this point with the Confessor but the door has been sealed, it is indistinguishable from all the other doors of the center, the murmuring of confessions through the poorly soundproofed alcoves all up and down the corridor makes it impossible for me to know where or which my Confessor is and thus there is nothing to do but to talk away. Even if I were to blunder into the wrong room to share these confidences, I would get the same answer anyway. No less than the technicians themselves the Confessors have been carefully ordered and the procedural manuals would apply.

Nonetheless I feel somewhat relieved; confession has been a positive step and I have the assurances of the technicians if not of my companion that I am acting properly and in accord with the imperatives of this difficult society. I would have it no other way; it was not rebelliousness which sent me this way but the need to assimilate, I must ferret out my own condition in order to properly integrate. If this were not so, I know, they never would have permitted me in the machinery at all, never allowed me the hypnotics to penetrate the programs.

On the great and empty desert he takes himself to see the form of Satan, manifest in the guise of an itinerant, wandering amidst the sands. Moving with an odd, off-center gait, rolling on limping claw, Satan seems eager for the encounter and he is ready for it too, ready at last to wrestle the old, damned angel and be done with it, but Satan is taking his time—the cunning of the creature—and seems ever reluctant to make the encounter. Perhaps he is merely being taunted. Once again he thinks of the odd discrepancy of persona; he is unable in this particular role to work within the first person but is instead a detached observer seeing all of it at a near and yet far remove, imprisoned within the perception, yet unable to affect. An interesting phenemenon, perhaps he has some fear that to become the persona would be blasphemous. He will have to discuss this too with the technicians. Then again, maybe not. Maybe he will not discuss it with the technicians; it is none of their damned business, any of it, and besides he has all that he can do to concentrate upon Satan who in garb of bright hues and dull comes upon him.

"Are you prepared?" Satan says. He has a pleasant, confident voice. "Are you ready for the undertaking?"

He looks down at his sandals embedded in the dense and settled sands. "Yes," he says, "I am ready now."

"Do you know the consequences?" Satan's voice

is quite ingratiating, a warm and personal manner here, an offhand ease which enjoins distrust but then again this would have been expected. What belies the manner, however, is the face, the riven and broken features, the darting aspect of the eyes, the small crevices in which torment and desert sweat lurk and which compel attention beyond the body which has been broken by the perpetration of many seeming injustices.

Satan extends his arm. "Let's wrestle," he says.

"Non disputandum," he says. "I understood first that we were to talk and only then to struggle."

"Latin is no protection here," Satan says firmly. "All tongues pay homage to me. I can be prayed to through all the devices; there are words for me throughout the universe."

"Mais non," he says, trying his abominable French. "Voulez-vous je me porte bien?"

"Nor does humor exist in this open space," Satan says. "From walking up and down upon the earth and to and fro upon it I have learned the emptiness of present delight. Come," he says, leaning forward, his arm extended, "let us wrestle now."

He reaches for that gnarled limb but brings his hands back. The sun is pitiless overhead but like a painting: he does not feel the heat. His only physical sensation is of the dry and terrible odor seeping from his antagonist. "No," he says, "mais non, mon frere. Not until we have had the opportunity to speak."

"There is nothing about which to speak. There

21

are no sophistries in this emptiness, merely conten-
tion."

Do not argue with Satan. He had been warned of
this, had known it as his journey toward the
darkness had begun, had known that there was no
way in which the ancient and terrible enemy could
be engaged by dialetic and yet, *non disputandum,* he
has failed again. Not to do it. Not to try argument;
it is time to wrestle and it might as well be done.

He seizes the wrist. Slowly, he and Satan lock.

Coming to grips with that old antagonist, it is to
the man as if he has found not an enemy but only
some long-removed aspect of himself, as if indeed,
just as in sex or dreams, he is in the act of complet-
ing himself with this engagement. The stolidity of
the form, the interlock of limbs gives him not a
sense of horror as he might have imagined but,
rather, comfort. It must have been this way. Their
hands fit smoothly together. "Do you see?" Satan
says winking and coming to close quarters. "You
know that it must always have been meant this
way. Touch me my friend, touch and find grace."
Slowly, evenly, Satan begins to drag him forward.

He understands, he understands what is happening to him: Satan in another of his guises would
seduce him with warmth when it is really a mask
for evil. He should be fighting against the ancient
and terrible enemy with renewed zeal for recog-
nizing this, but it is hard, it is hard to do so when
Satan is looking at him with such compassion,
when the mesh of their bodies is so perfect. Never
has he felt anyone has understood him this well; his
secret and most terrible agonies seem to flutter, one

by one, birdlike across the features of the antagonist and he could if he would sob out all of his agonies knowing that Satan could understand. Who would ever understand as well? It must have been the same for Him.

I do not want to believe, he means to cry out to Satan, I believe none of it; I am taken by strange, shrieking visions and messages in the night; I feel that I must take upon the host of Heaven and yet these dreams which leave me empty and sick are madness, I hear the voice speaking unto me saying I am the Father, I am the incompleteness which you will fill and know that this too must be madness and yet I cannot deny that voice, can deny no aspect of it which is what set me here upon the desert, but I am filled with fear and trembling . . . he wants to cry out all of this to Satan but he will not, he will not, and slowly he finds himself being drawn to the ground.

"Comfort," Satan says in the most confiding and compassionate of whispers, covering him now with his gnarled body so that the sun itself is obscured, all landscape dwindled to the small perception of shifting colors, "comfort: I understand, I am your dearest and closest friend. Who can ever understand you as I? Who would possibly know your anguish. Easy, be easeful," Satan says and he begins to feel the pressure across his chest. "So easy," Satan murmurs, "it will be so easy for only I understand; we can dwell together," and breath begins to desert him. The devil is draining his respiration.

Understanding that, he understands much else:

the nature of the engagement, the quality of deception, exactly what has been done to him. Just as Satan was the most beautiful and best-loved of all the angels, so in turn he would be Satan's bride in the act of death. It is the kiss that will convey the darkness, and seeing this he has a flickering moment of transcendence: he thinks he knows now how he might be able to deal with this. Knowing the devil's meaning will enable him to contest, and yet it would be so easy—inevitable is the word, necessary—to yield to his antagonist and let it be done, let the old, cold, bold intruder have his will, thy will be done and Satan's too and the yielding is so close to him now he can feel himself leaning against the network of his being, the empty space where desire might have rested, in the interstices the lunge toward annihilation—mais non, he says, mais non, je renounce, I will not do it!—and forces himself against the figure, understanding finally the nature of this contest, what it must accomplish, in what mood it must be done and wearily, wearily, carrying all of consequence upon him he begins the first and final of all his contests with the devil.

"Why don't you curse God and die?" his wife, who looks like Edna, says to him conversationally. "This can't go on much longer this way." Stench from the diseased and dying cattle wafts into quarters. "Don't you think you've had quite enough of this?"

Job picks absently at one of his boils, looking at her compressed little features; never is his wife so certain as at moments of renunciation. Surely he could have perceived this a long time ago but crisis brings out the center. "There must be a reason for this," he says calmly, "the Lord giveth and the Lord taketh away. Naked came I into this world—"

"That's a pack of bullshit," his wife screams. She flings a rolled up sock at him. "You know better than that; you're just making excuses."

Job shrugs. The Comforters have not prepared him for confrontations of this sort. Their advice has been useful but largely of a metaphysical order and his wife, as he should have suspected all along, is no metaphysician. He walks to the open window, stares out at the desolate fields; the thin, extinguishing fires wafting odors of desiccation. "There must be a reason for all of this, a grander design," he says, "and in due course all will come clear."

His wife does not answer this. She is a deeply embittered woman as she has every right to be under these circumstances and he really should have expected no different. He thinks of what has been done to him, the test which has been imposed, the intolerable difficulties which have been conjoined with circumstance as a test of faith and a strange thought occurs to him, one which he would not have calculated to have struck him at this time: why do I think the Lord is behind all of this, Job muses? Or for that matter why even credit Satan? Perhaps it is merely circumstance; perhaps there is no motive, perhaps there is no reason at all.

Perhaps it is merely an occurrence upon which

he is imputing causation and it means nothing at all.

Nothing at all.

It is a madly technocratic age, an age of cool wires and distant targets and yet it is not cruel: the devices of our existence, we have been assured, exist only in order to perpetrate our being. Remove the technology and the planet would kill us, take away the institutions and the technology would collapse. There is no way in which we can continue to be supported without the technology and the institutions and furthermore they are essentially benign.

They are benign. This is neither rationalization nor an attempt to conceal from myself and others the dreadful aspects of our mortality, the engines of our condition grinding us slowly, slowly away . . . no, this is a fixed and rational judgement which comes from a true assessment of the times.

It is true that a hundred years ago, in the decades of the great slaughters and even beyond the institutions were characterized by vengeance, pusillanimity, murder and fear but no more. In 2160 the oligarchy was finally toppled and the reordering began. By 2189, the very year in which I was born, the slaughter was already glimpsed within historical context. I was nurtured by a reasonable state in a reasonable fashion; if I needed love I found it: sustenance was there in more forms than the purely physical. I grew within the bounds of the state; indeed, I matured to a full and reasonable compassion. Aware of the limits which were imposed I did not resent them nor find them stifling.

There was space; there has been space for a long time now. Standing on the high parapet of the dormer, looking out on Intervalley Six and the web of connecting arteries beneath the veil of dust, I can see the small lights of the many friendly cities nodding and winking in the darkness, the penetrating cast of light creating small spokes of fire moving upward in the night. Toward the west the great thrust of South Harvest rears its bulk and spires, lending geometry to a landscape which would otherwise be endless, and I find reassurance in that presence just as I find reassurance in the act of being on the parapet itself. There was a time and it was not so terribly long ago that they would not have allowed residents to stand out on the parapet alone; the threat of suicide was constant but in the last years the statistics have become increasingly favorable, and it is now within the means of all of us, if only we will to come out in the night for some post-industrial air.

Edna is beside me. For once we are not talking; our relationship has become almost endlessly convoluted now, filled with despair, rationalization and dialogue but in simple awe of the vision she too has stopped talking and it is comfortable, almost companionable to stand with her thus, our hands touching lightly, smelling the strange little breezes of our technology. A long time ago people went out in pairs to places like this and had a kind of emotional connection triggered by the solitude and the vision but now emotions are reserved for more sensible areas like the hypnotics. Nevertheless, it is pleasant to stand with her thus. It would almost be possible for me at this moment to conceive some genuine attachment to her except that I know better; it is not the union but its absence which tantalizes me at this moment, the knowledge that there is no connection which will ever mean as much as this landscape. The sensation is unbearably poignant although it does not match in poignance other moments I have had under the hypnotics.

At length, Edna turns toward me, her touch more tentative in the uneven light and says, "It hurts me too. It hurts all of us in about the same way."

"I wasn't really thinking about pain."

"Still," she says, "listen, pain is the constant for all of us. Some can bear it and others cannot. Some can face this on their own terms and others need artificial means of sustention. There is really nothing to be done."

"I don't *need* artificial means. That was a choice; I have a goal which can only be accomplished."

"Surely," she says quietly, "absolutely."

"And they're not artificial."

She shrugs, looks out toward the light. "Everything is artificial, Harold."

They are not, I want to say. The experiences under the hypnotics are as real, as personally viable, as much the blocks of personality formulation as anything which this confused and dim woman can offer, as anything which has passed between us. But that would only lead to another of our arguments and I feel empty of the need for confrontation. Deep below we can hear the uneven cries of the simulacrum animals let out at last for the evening zoo, the intermingled, troubled roars of tigers, the chatterings of primates strung by wire, the murmurings of birds triggered by electron passages.

"Has it made any difference?" she says, "any of it?"

"Any of what? I don't understand."

"The treatments," she says. "You've been in them but have they changed you? Is everything changed or have you only found yourself over and again?"

Tantalized, I find myself on the verge of a comment which will anneal everything but, as is so often the case, it slips from me and I say, "Of course they have made a difference."

"What have you gained?"

"Pardonne? Pardonze moi?"

"Don't be obscure with me, Harold, that may work with the clinicians but it doesn't matter to me. I want the truth."

"Why? What does truth matter?"

"Can't you answer that?"

"I have no easy answers."

"Tell me anyway."

"Merde," I say quietly. My tendency to lapse into weak French under stress is an old disability, even before the hypnotics, still, I have never quite become accustomed to it. Her predecessors have never put me under the stress that Edna does. "I don't know," I say, "I think there's been a difference, yes. If I didn't believe that I'd stop now."

"Well you're ready to quit, then. It's done nothing at all. You're the same."

"Let's go inside now," I say. "It's cold."

"You're the *same*. Only more withdrawn, a little more stupid. You've lost any edge of force. And these treatments are supposed to heal?"

Prosthetic dogs bark. "No, they merely broaden. Healing comes from within. All of us understand that."

"Broaden! You understand less than ever."

I put a hand to my face, feel the little webbing where not so many years from now the deep lines will be, the grooves of life burnt in. "Let's go inside," I say again. "There's nothing more to say out here."

"Why don't you face the truth? These treatments are not meant to help you; they are meant to make you more stupid so that you won't cause any trouble. That's what they developed them for, so people like you with a high intensity level would just retreat into dreams, not do anything to shake the structure—"

I move away from her. "It doesn't matter," I say. "None of it matters. It is of no substance whatsoever. Why do you insist that it must be otherwise?" I walk toward the funnel. "The significance is what we impute," I say. It is the voice of the technician. "Someday you will see that."

There is nothing for her to do but follow. She would argue if we were to stay by the parapet, she would fight on and on if the position were held but my withdrawal has offered the most devastating answer of all: I simply do not care. The attitude is not simulated. On the most basic level I refuse to interact.

"You are a fool," she says, crowding against me for the drop. "You do not understand what they are doing to you. You simply do not care."

"Quite right," I say, "quite right. Absolutely. Not at all. That is the point now, isn't it?"

The light ceases.

We plunge.

Dreaming, I make intersection, the slow and certain conjoinment, the dark weld. As if from a great distance I hear birdlike cries, ornaments to my necessity as I work within her, the whisk of sheets, slow thump of the boards to augment that rising and the clarity of the defeat which must follow. Fluid against fluid, pressure against purchase and then I am free, vaulted above her in that clean, five second flight before the drop and she tolerates it all, takes of it what she can and must as blindly I scuttle back toward the cage. I fall on top of her moaning and for a long time the cool expulsion of her breath against me is all that I feel. "This is freedom?" she says to me at last, *"This?"* I do not answer. There is nothing to say. "This is not freedom," she says. She takes my hand, leads it to her, slowly I work against the panels of her own circumstance. "There," she says and "there," again and I do what I can, what I must, the light of the room overtaking and this second conjoinment has more ferocity, more authority than the first as I slide her over and the reason for this must be, there can be no other, that this time I do not escape myself.

Cold, cold, bound within myself I observe her with a clinician's care as she works her way to and past fury, twists, gurgles and then lies beside me. Still inside, I shift, push my way clear and then am released.

"Freedom?" I say, "is this freedom?"

She says nothing.

"Edna," I say, "there is no freedom at all."

I am in an ashram, surrounded by incense and the dull outlines of those who must be my followers. Clumped in the darkness, they listen to me chant. It is a mantra which I appear to be singing in a high, cracked chant; it resembles the chanting of the Lubavitchers of Bruck Linn, although far more regularized in the vocal line, and limited in sound. *Om* or *ay* or *eeh;* the sounds are interchangeable and I am more than willing to accept the flow of it, not rationalize, not attempt to control those sounds but rather to let them issue according to my mood.

It is peaceful here and I am deeply locked within myself; the soft breath of my followers lends resonance to the syllables which indeed seem to assume a more profound meaning but at a certain point there is commotion and the sound of doors crashing and then in the strophes of light I can see that the room has been invaded by what appear to be numerous members of the opposition. They are wearing their dull attack uniforms, even if nothing else I can perceive that in the difficult light. From the glint of weaponry I can see that this is very serious. They move with an awful tread into the room, half a dozen of them, and then the portable incandescence is turned. We are pinned in frieze.

I know that it is going to be very bad. The acts of 2013 outlawed exactly what is going to happen here, the pogroms have dwindled to harassment, random, isolated incursions. But now and then there are terrible outbreaks, uncontrollable reversions and I know that this is what will happen here; persecution runs in the blood; I know the machinery of disorder. Until this moment I did not think that they would move upon me in this abandoned church in the burnt-out core of the devastated city but my luck, it seems, has suddenly, convulsively run out. I always knew that it would. Surely in some corner of the heart I have known this: the *om* must always have been energized by doom.

But it is one thing to consider demolition in a corner of the heart and another, quite, to live it. Job loved God, trusted in His mercy, abandoned himself to His judgement but all of that was before the cattle began to drop and the lands quickly to wither; Job's faith was constant only at remove as he, to his disgrace, discovered. Martyrdom is easy to consider in the abstract; martyrdom is tears and the ripping of the bowels when it is incurred; the splenous rending is not to be associated with grace.

"Abdul," one of them says pointing, his finger enormous, dazzling and as I lift my eyes to it I feel myself subsiding in the wickers of light, "Abdul you are in violation of the codes and you will pay for it."

"I am not in violation," I say, trying to preserve

a kind of calm. "I am entitled to free exercise. Surely you know this as well as I. We have been granted freedom—"

They begin to laugh. "Freedom for one is freedom for the group," the speaker says, "We will investigate the degree of this for all."

In a moment they will plunge toward me. They hold the instant timeless, enjoying it. I know how it goes then and what will happen: they will strike at me with their weapons and bring me to a posture of contrition; they will obliterate consciousness and cause bloodstains; not of the least importance they will humiliate me before my small congregation which has already witnessed enough humiliation, thank you very much, otherwise why would they have gathered? They control the time and it is theirs.

I can tolerate all of that, I suppose. I have dreamed worse, not to say suffered many privations and indignities before opening this little subunit. The liberating acts of 2013 gave me, I thought, the chance like everyone else to make my way in the world; I was willing to take the chance, a little martyrdom might even have been considered good for business. None of that concerns me, what does, I must admit, is the fear that I will show weakness before my congregation. To be humiliated is one thing but to show fear, beg for mercy, is quite another: I would hardly be able to deal with it. A religious man must put up a stiff front. A religious man whose cult is based upon the regular, monotonic articulation of ancient chants in a search for inner serenity can hardly be seen quivering and shrieking in front of those who have come for tranquility.

They have come for tranquility; I cannot give them chaos. That is the pact that existence has made for them but which religion was created to shelter.

Thinking this I resolve to be steadfast, to draw myself to full stature or what there is left of it after all these years of controlled diet and deliberate physical mutilation. "You will not prevail," I say. "You cannot prevail against the forces of the om," and with a hand signal I indicate to my congregation that I wish to resume the chant, humiliate the attackers if I can by my own transcendence. But they do not attend. Indeed, they do not attend at all, so eager do so many of them appear to search out any means of exit available. They are a weak and battered group, dysfunction and covert rage took them to the ashram, how could I expect them to stand and fight? A small alley has been left open through the ranks of the massed opposition leading to one of the doors and in their unseemly haste to clear the hall they ignore me. Religious disposition, it would seem, is a function of boredom, at least for my congregation: give people something really necessary to face in their lives and religion can be ignored, except by the fanatics who consider religion itself important, of course, but they are disaster-ridden.

Like flies these little insights buzz about, gnawing and striking small pieces of psychic flesh while the hall is emptied. My congregation, aged and crippled, is permitted to hobble out, the invaders have obviously no interest in them whatsoever. Congregants are not to be implicated; to bear witness is certainly not to incur responsibility. The sting of the insights is not prophylactic, no asepsis; they do no good whatsoever. If anything they can be said to magnify my sense of helplessness. To know is perhaps to incur paralysis; it is only self-delusion which grants one the possibility of free will. This would be an apt subject for a homily if I were to believe that there was any future in organized religion for me. At the present time it does me little good.

"Gentlemen," I say, raising a hand after the last congregant has scuttled out, the door flapping like a banner, "this is a futile business. Join me in a chant. Let us all humble ourselves for reason and sacrifice."

I kneel; my forehead near the floor and begin to mumble, hoping that the intensity of this commitment will strike shame within them, convince them that they are dealing with someone so dangerously self-absorbed that all of their attacks would be futile, but even as I commence the syllables I am pulled to my feet by a man in a uniform which I do not recognize; he must have come in later, a supervisor. He stares at me from a puffy, heart-shaped face and then raises his hand, strikes me skillfully across first one cheek and then the other. The collision of flesh is enormous; I feel as if I am spattering within. No one ever indicated, even in the sacred texts, that there could be so much pain in it.

"You're a fool," he says, "a fool to have done this."

"I was allowed. Statutes proffer—"

"Ignore the statutes. For your own sake, your own possibility, why did you do this?"

"Why do you care?" I say. I am quite frightened. Power unmasked is quite terrifying; liturgy is no preparation. "Why are you asking this? What is it to you?"

He hits me again. No progression of the sacred blocks of personality, the levels of eminent reason have prepared me for this kind of pain. I begin to cry in a child's bleating voice. It is quite humiliating. "Please," I mumble, "don't do it again. The pain is dreadful, I can't take it—"

"Some martyr," the supervisor says. The troops laugh. He seizes me by the hair. "Give me a response," he says, "don't withdraw, don't protest, don't argue; it will lead only to more blows and eventually the same outcome. Simply answer the questions and it will go much easier for both of us. Knowing all the penalties, knowing of the responsibility you must take for your acts and what would happen, why did you nonetheless persist? Didn't you understand? Didn't you know what danger you brought not only upon yourself but the fools you seduced? Now they too will have to pay."

"The statutes permitted me to open the ashram, to have a congregation."

"That is true. But you forget the other part, don't you? They also permit persecution. 2013 let options into our lives. What went for you went for us; you were free to worship but we were free to kill."

Free to kill. Yes, that is true; I had severed it

from consciousness but that is exactly right. The need for prayer is counterbalanced by the urge to destroy; I was aware of that but never regarded it as relevant. "Why kill?" I say. A drop of blood falls from my face; astonished we stare at it. "Why kill when you can pray?"

"Some need to do the one," the leader says, "and some the other." He is, I can see, choleric with rage; his face seems to have inflated not only with blood but reason as he stands there and I begin to comprehend that he is suffering from more than situational stress. Looking at him I want to accentuate that sudden feeling of bonding but there is every emotion save sympathy in that ruined face. "Listen, now, attend to me—"

He hits me again, convulsively. This is the most painful blow yet because I thought I had reached him. I fall and begin to weep. The bones of my face seem welded. This is no proper action for a martyr but I never wanted it to be this way: I never thought that there could be such blood in sacrifice. He puts one strong hand under an arm, drags me grunting to my feet, positions me in front of him as if I were a statue.

"Do you know what we're going to have to do now?" he says, "we're going to have to make an example of you, you dirty praying swine, that's all. We're going to have to kill you. Why did you put us in this position?"

"You won't do it," I say weakly.

"Yes we will."

"Not here. You couldn't. Not in the temple; you wouldn't *want* to do it—"

"This is not a temple. It is a dirty, cluttered room and you are an old fool who imagines it to be a church."

"Om," I say. The word comes. I did not calculate this. "Om eeh. Ay."

"You would fight us regardless. If the state believed in om you would cry for freedom of choice. If the state were stateless you would wish to form institutions. There is no hope for you people, none at all. You would be aberrants in any culture at any time and you cannot understand this. You wish to be isolated, persecuted, to die, and it has *nothing* to do with religion." He leans over, stares at me, his eyes curiously mournful. *"We* uphold religion," he says, "we are committed to the order which you in your apostasy and simple greed would destroy. We have been licensed to clean you out just as you have been licensed to decay."

"Eeh. Ay. Oooh. Ahh. Om."

"Enough of this."

"Ai," I say. "Om, oy."

"Enough of it," he said, and he signals to the others behind him. They approach slowly, reluctantly but with gathering speed as they close in, perhaps catching a whiff of prophecy which comes from the syllables. "You wish a public death, you wish martyrdom, then you will certainly have it. Reports will be issued to all of the provinces. Icons will be constructed. Dispatches will even glorify. You will achieve everything that you were unable in life. But this will do you no good whatsoever."

"Om," I say, "Oh."

For the fear is tightly controlled now. Truly, the

syllables work. I would not have granted them such efficacy and yet what I have advised my congregants all this time turns out to be true. They paste over the sickness with the sweeter contaminants of courage, grant purchase upon terror, make it possible for the most ignorant and cowardly of men which must be myself to face annihilation with constancy and grace.

"Om," I say, "eeh. If it were to be done, then it would be done quickly."

"Ah," he says, "now you speak."

"Do it quickly."

"It is impossible," he says. "Nothing will be gained from this and yet you still will not face the truth. It would be so much easier if at least you would give up your bankrupt purchase, if you would understand that you are dying for no reason whatsoever and that it could have been no other way. It would make matters so much easier if you simply would stop *deluding* yourself—"

"Ah. Oh."

"Oh, shit," the man with the heart-shaped face says and gives a signal to one of the troops who closes upon me, a small man in uniform with a high calibered weapon. Its cold surfaces meld to my temple. I can feel the shaking of his hand, the quiver against the ridged veins, not perceived but taken. "Is this right?" the man in uniform says, "is this how I should hold it?"

"You couldn't get it in any deeper," I say. It is remarkable how I have gained in courage and detachment; just an instant ago it would have seemed impossible and here I am demonstrating even a certain insouciance. I appear ready to face what I feared the most with implacable ardor. Is it the power of the chant or simply that I do not believe that this is happening? That I lie dreaming under machinery and that at the appropriate time wires will be disconnected and I will be asked to move again?

"Now," the leader says. "Do it now."

"At once?"

"Instantly."

There is a pause of the greatest implication. *Om* resonates through me, I subvocalize, clench my fists. It will be that with which I will die, it will carry me directly to the outermost curved part of the universe. I close my eyes, waiting for the transport but it does not come and, so quickly, I understand that it will not. Something has happened, either to the machinery or to the situation. Reasonable passage seems to have been denied. I stare. The positions are the same except that the leader has moved away some paces to protect against recoil and the man carrying the gun is biting his lip. Tears are on his cheeks much as they were on mine.

"Shoot him you fool," the leader says. "Why aren't you doing this? What's wrong with you?"

"I am having difficulty—"

"*Kill* him, you bastard."

"That's the problem. I can't seem to."

"You can't *seem* to?"

There is another long pause. I flutter my eyes. Om has receded. "I can't," the man with the gun says finally. "I can't put him down like an animal, just put a bullet into his brain. This isn't what I was prepared to do. You didn't say that it would be this way; you said that there would be resistance, that they would be waiting for us with weaponry. I was prepared for combat, not murder. Isn't that right, mates?" He turns toward the others. "We were asked to go into battle here, not to work in the slaughtering docks. I say that we shouldn't have any part of it."

"Ah shit," the heart-shaped man says again, "shit." He comes toward us, breaks the connection with a swipe of his hand, knocking down the gun arm and the supporter goes scuttling away. Troops murmur. The leader looks at me with hatred, red-tinted veins alight. "You think you've proven something," he says, "but you've proven absolutely nothing. Weakness is weakness. You're making me do it myself, that's all and it isn't enough."

I shrug. It is all that I can do to maintain my demeanor considering the exigencies but I have done it. "Om," I murmur. Ripples of quietude expand; the pool of self murmurs. Transparent it glows back at me, reflects my own wise and penitent features. "It was all permitted under the statutes," I point out. "It falls well within the procedural. Om."

"Om," he says, "om yourself." He removes a weapon, caresses it with one hand, then puts it against my temple. "Very well," he says, "it could have been easier but instead it will be more complex. That does not matter. All that matters is consummation; that is why we were detailed."

"Consummate. Om."

"I don't want to do this," he says with a sudden,

immense confidentiality. "I hope you understand. It's nothing personal; I have little against you, it's just a matter of assignment, of the social roles we occupy." Unlike the others he seems to need to prepare himself for assassination through a massive act of disconnection. "Nothing personal," he says mildly.

"Everything's personal. Study the texts."

"Really? I don't believe that."

"You'd have to devote years to the sacred writings to know that. But it's true."

"It may well be. Still, it doesn't change the situation, does it now?" The kindness in his voice is immense. He has become a changed assassin in a matter of moments. The act must be portentous; it blunts or at least changes the force of the will.

"I don't know," I say. "I don't want to die particularly. Still, I seem able to face it."

And this to be sure is the truth. Calm percolates from the center of the corpus through the very brain stem: I seem awash in dispassion. Perhaps it is the knowledge that this is all a figment, that it is a dream. I believe in the technicians now; I believe that I will awaken to sterile encosure and their greeting. "Do it," says the man. "Go ahead and do it."

Could this be the secret of all the martyrs? That at the very end of it, past flesh and panic, they knew they would awaken to the voice of the machines? This is very possibly the explanation for all the acts of heroism, the testaments of those who were truly great: they knew that they could not die. On the other hand, maybe not. Maybe none of this

43

is so. Like everything else it is difficult and complex. Still, it can be met with a reasonable amount of dignity which is all that any one of us can ask.

"Indeed," he says softly, "indeed, indeed. I want you to know that you have my greatest admiration, however; you're being splendid about this."

I smile and incline my head in modest thanks. Meanwhile, he fires the gun into my temple, killing me at once and precipitating in that one jagged bolt the great religious riots and revivals of the early twenties and not a moment too soon, the movement needed the impetus and the martyrdom, Allah and all of the minor prophets be praised. Be praised, be praised.

"You won't get rid of me so easily," the snake says, coiling his tail and chewing delicately on a leaf, "I'll be back by the end of Revelations to be sure. I have big plans; you can't bring a banishment so easily."

"Look at them," I say gesturing. "Look what you've done." Even as they coil yet again in rut I begin to shake with anger. "And it could have been so beautiful," I say.

"Don't be ridiculous," the snake says pleasantly. "You wouldn't have known what to do with the circumstance. It's chaos, polarities, the disjunction of opposites for which you survive; you wouldn't have gone to the trouble otherwise." He rolls to and fro upon the earth, merrily. "Out of the void, forms," he says. "How else could you replicate?"

"You tease me with sophistry."

"Sophistry is another word for unbearable truth.

Come on," the snake says seductively, "pat my belly, scratch me about the ears, come and roll on the ground with me for a while. It won't hurt at all and might give you some respite. Let us play. We're going to go on like this through eternity and wind up in the same condition at Revelation anyway so we might as well enjoy ourselves."

I look at him in disgust; images of the fervid scene below casting his aspect in revulsion. "It isn't that way at all," I say, "it isn't play but fate."

"You love the disorder, the ambivalence and the chaos. Who would know better than I?"

"*You* love them."

"Ah," he says, "that is true and the only difference between us is that I admit it while you're still trying to put another face on the matter. But that will change."

"Everything will change."

"Everything will stay the same. But your attitude will change and you will even come to enjoy this."

"Enjoy it?" I say, shocked, "how could you possibly think that I will come to enjoy it?"

"Wait until Job," he says, "just hang on through the Chronicles and you'll see."

I stare at him astonished.

"You always have, you know," he says.

Systematically I face examination in the cold room. It is a necessary part of the procedure, a central fact of policy. The only hint of the portentousness of the events I have lived is the small mark on my wrist. "There is very little depersonalization," I say, "it crept into the last of the Ashram segment,

I admit, but it only really occurs often in the Jesus episodes. I seem unable to occupy that role within the first person but feel the disassociative reaction of which you spoke. I seem to be witnessing him as if from the outside without really having control over the actions."

The Counselor nods. "This is highly charged and emotional material. Obviously. Disassociative reaction is common in such cases, even without schizoid background; many who showed no signs tend to depersonalize. That in itself is not ominous. Of course, at some point in your life you must have had a Jesus fixation; that's taken for granted here."

"Not so," I say. "In fact I did not know who he was until I was introduced to the texts. All of this material is unfamiliar to me; I deliberately wanted something which would be outside of my experience."

"Surely it hit some responsive chord."

"I wouldn't know about that at all."

"In any case, I wouldn't be unduly concerned. That in itself is no reason for panic, we're satisfied. As you continue to integrate into the persona it will fall away and you will begin to actively participate in the events."

"I already do."

"I mean, all of the time," the Counselor says, "you'll no longer detach yourself at critical moments."

"I don't know about that," I say. "I feel no special emotional reaction to the material; it's the same as any of the others. In fact, it's inexplicable."

"I tell you," the Counselor says with a touch of irritation, "that is of no concern here. The process is self-reinforcing. What concerns us are your over-all reactions, the gross medical signs, the question of organic imbalance. The psycho reactions will fall into place if we control the somatic."

Somatic. Psychic. Congenital. Disassociation. I think of all of their words, the words of their testimony which they use to embrace the process and for all I know kill it as I stare past him at the walls of the room which contain schematic portraits of the intervalley network. Interspersed are various documents certifying the authenticity of his role as an observer. The absence of abstract material disturbs me; until now it had never occurred to me how deprived our institutions seem to be of the evidence of art but now it does. The hypnotics must be working. Clearly, I hunger for something more than a schematic response to our condition; I am looking for symbols, metaphor, a kind of beauty. This design does not make me contemptible.

"Are you listening to me?" he says. "Did you hear the question just now?"

"No, I guess I didn't."

He shakes his head. "I am going to administer a gross verbal reaction test. Are you ready?"

"Ready for what? A test? Why is that necessary? I am in excellent contact, you said so yourself."

"That is a judgement which can only be fully investigated by the test. I am sure everything will be excellent."

"Then why bother?"

"That is a judgement which falls under the policies and procedures of the institute."

"Must you? Why?"

"We must; we wish to guard against exactly that which you manifest which strikes me as a rather hostile, detached response. We do not encourage this kind of side effect, you see; we consider it a negative aspect of treatment."

"That's regrettable."

"It is sometimes necessary to terminate treatment in the face of such reactions, so I would not be so flippant. That could be interpreted as part of disassociation."

"Why do you do this to us?" I say. I look at his bland pleasant face, masked by institutional sheen but nonetheless concealing, I am convinced, as passionate and confused a person as I might be, perhaps a person even more passionate and confused since he has not had, after all, the benefit of the treatments. "Why cannot we simply go through this on our own terms, take what we can take, miss the rest of it? Why must we be so closely monitored?"

"The procedures demand exactly that."

"Don't tell me of procedures," I say, leaning forward with a sudden intensity, aware that I am twitching at the joints and extremities in a new fashion, emotionally moved as has rarely been the case. Clearly the treatments are affecting me, I must accept their position to that point. "The real reason is that you're afraid that unless we're controlled we might really be *changed,* that we might react in a fashion that you couldn't predict, that we wouldn't be studying *religion* and *fanaticism* any more but would actually become religious fanatics and what would you make of us then?"

"Confinement cases," the Confessor says flatly. "For your own protection. Which is exactly what we want to avoid by the process of what you call monitoring which we know to be a mere certification that you are in condition to continue the treatments. Without doing damage to yourself."

"Or to the state."

"Of course to the state. I work for it, you live within it, why should we not have the interests of the state at heart? The state need not be perceived as the enemy by you people, you know. The state is a neutral constant, essentially benign as you ought to know or these treatments would not be available."

"I made no comment on the state."

"You can't make us the repository of all your difficulties, the rationalizing force for your inadequacies. The state is a positive force in all of your lives and you have more personal freedom than any citizenry at any time in the history of the world. What you take for granted was the subject of resolutions. We crawled from brutality to arrive at this."

"I know the history," I say with some irritation. "I'm not ignorant."

"But you are; you consider yourself superior to us simply because you don't accept what the rest of us know to be worth accepting. In fact," the Counselor goes on, rising, his face suffused now with what might be passion but then on the other hand might only be the consequence of improper diet, highly spiced intake, the slow closure of the arteries, arteriosclerosis being one of the untreatable diseases of all post-technology, "in fact we can get damned sick of you people and your attitudes. I'm no less human than you because I have a bureaucratic job, I want you to know that; I have the same problems that you do. The only difference is that I'm trying to spply myself toward constructive purposes while what you want is irresponsibility to get out."

He wipes a hand across his streaming features, shrugs, sits again. "Sorry to overreact," he says, "It's just that a good deal of frustration builds within us functionaries and it has to be expressed. This isn't easy for any of us, you know. We're people just as you are; we have interiors, we suffer, we're trying to come to terms with this unspeakable age no less than you. Maybe our way of doing it doesn't appeal to you but no more does yours appeal to us; what we're talking about is dignity, the transaction of humanity—" He stops talking, opens a drawer, takes out a spool of computer tape and wipes his forehead. "An extra," he says. "What do you think; we don't have pressures just like you? We can't crawl into the machines and get away; that option's denied us."

There seems little to say. I could point out that this is his choice, not mine, but it would lead only to another tirade and I want to get out of this interview as quickly as possible. For all I know his fury might be part of the evaluation process. I consider certain texts which give the value of the absorption of provocation without replying in kind and remain quietly in my chair, thinking of this and that and many other things having to do with the monitoring conducted by these institutions and what it might suggest about the nature of interrelation but thought is increasingly repulsive to me. What I concentrate upon, what I seek, what I hoped that the process might give me, is feeling and it is that which I will cultivate. "I'm ready for the test," I say mildly.

"Test? Oh yes. Very good." The Counselor folds the tape around its spool tightly, puts it back in the desk. "Time to proceed. Just a series of questions which I would like you to answer as briefly and straightforwardly as possible." His tone is amiable; humility casts him in a pacific light. "Just the first response that comes to you."

"Certainly," I say, echoing his calm. "Tres bonne, merci. Maintenant et pourquoi."

"Pourquoi?" he says vaguely. "Pourquoi?"

"I don't *know* pourquoi," I say.

"We *can* change," Edna says. Her pained eyes open to depths of luminescence. "We backslide, governments fail us, our leaders betray, our hopes fall away but in infinitesmal ways the human soul, the heart can be taught to apprehend. It is different now than it used to be. People are kinder, warmer, more open, more vulnerable, quicker to touch."

Edna sips from her glass of bitters, a faint tremor in her delicate hand. In deference to the treatments I am drinking water but no anodynes could give me the passion that I feel now. Her expressiveness is to me the most adored part of her even though from the wastes of my own dread, I fear that her optimism comes from naivete. Robomechanisms drift by us on skates, the thin hum of the support systems fills the cafe. An old man in the corner nods, screams, flails desperately and is on the instant trapdoored; the odors of his failure persist with those of spinach greens. Our robowaiter, observing my discomfort is at our table immediately. "Not to worry sir, not to worry," he says. "His time was approaching; he was sustained here by the comforts of the state longer than would have been true otherwise." He adopts a Counselor's posture, his features reddening with intentness as circuits closed. "Will there be any more?" he says. "This can be on the courtesy of the state." At other tables scattered through the lounge, other robowaiters are at tables making similar offers. It is possible to believe in the benignity of the institutions at this moment although I certainly do not."

"I will have some more white liquor," Edna says. "I would like water again," I say. The palliatives must be given up for the duration and I do so in good temper but white liquor would go now; the old man's self-destruction has left me feeling uneasy. But I dare not mask my feelings for Edna; even if the treatments were not a factor I would try to control my intake. We have known each other for only six months and in half of that I have been under the machines, but it is certainly the most profound relationship of my life. I have had sixteen affectionals and thirty-seven cooperatives altogether but none have ever been to me what Edna is; I am able to face this now and in that admission somehow have the strength to probe deeper. In and out of circumstance we have never known anything like this. She says that she feels the same. Everything that I say to her at this time she says back to me with greater force which is one of the reasons that I find her loveable; I am possessed of my own convictions. Some of them. Some of the time. "See the lovelies bleeding," Edna says as the waiter skates away for our state's gift, "see the century dreaming, see the hearts unknown." She coughs behind a palm. "You don't really *need* those treatments," she says, "do you now?"

"We have discussed this Edna. For the moment I need them. It is my election."

"Then we won't talk about it any more," she says agreeably. "You haven't been saying much. Are you all right?"

"I was listening to you."

"And thinking of the old man," she says cleverly. "Don't tell me you weren't."

"Not very much. A little, maybe. This kind of thing is still disturbing."

"He was a decompensate," she says, "and if it hadn't happened here it would have been somewhere else. Do you know what lovelies bleeding are?"

"No. You just mentioned them."

"I *know* I just mentioned them," she says a little irritably. The robowaiter skates back with the order, places it with a flourish and looks down upon us, his engine humming. "I think he wants to know if we want anything else," Edna says.

I look at the machine. "No," I say, "we want nothing else."

"That will be all then, sir," the machine says and

goes away. There are bumps underneath the floor. I do not want to think about what they mean.

"What are lovelies bleeding?" I say.

"A flower. A kind of flower. I looked it up in an old glossary; isn't that interesting?"

"Surely," I say, "it is all very interesting. Evocative." Screams from the corridors waft toward us; clearly it is the sound of the late afternoon detail reluctantly herding decompensates toward re-education and I wince with the troubling thought that too much of this is public nowadays. "A kind of flower," I say. "Life is a kind of flower, its blooms dying but exquisite."

"You're too pessimistic, O love. I told you that. You look for the worst interpretation, all the time. Things can get better; it's not the way it used to be. Back in the decade we took the decompensates for granted, never even tried to help them. Now there are details, re-education, synergy—"

"And treatments," I say.

"Not treatments. And you're not a decompensate, Harold; I wish you'd stop acting like one. Those who need help are being treated before they collapse."

"Surely," I say, "nonetheless the situation is itself fixed." I swallow some water. "I'm not as optimistic as you; there's a lot of pain now. And how benign is the state?"

"More than it was in the past. It takes time for things to change. It took *centuries* to arrive where we are and not everything can be solved at once."

"Perhaps," I say. I give a silent gesture. Despite the reforms and the attentions of the robowaiter it is still perhaps unwise to discuss the decompensates or the re-education details in the cafe. Edna, never stupid, brings her mouth to an *o* of understanding. "Or perhaps not."

"Perhaps we should leave," Edna says. "We could make love; we have the last twenty minutes of the shift left before I have to be in the mortuary and you have to prepare for your damned treatment. Making love would be nice." It is her disarming directness, her fragility, her astonishment at her own bluntness which makes her so loveable to me, the most profound of my sixteen affections. I am deeply stirred.

"Why not?" I say. I reach out to touch her hand. She caresses mine. In the fluorescence her hair is first brown, then red, shading toward fire, a little corona from her aspect although this may be my creation of desire. "Why not do that?" One of the robowaiters ruptures suddenly with a hollow sound; the explosion shakes the cafe. Plastics are thrown over him by the other machines, he is drenched with water and quickly rolled away.

"The sooner the better," I say. "My God, the sooner the very better."

"I wouldn't mention God, Harold," Edna says. She is not smiling. "Don't bring God into this too."

"All right," I say. I will not release her hand. I signal to our waiter. Shaken by the damage his fellow machine has incurred he skates over cautiously. I motion toward the check.

"Not to worry sir," he says, "not only the final round but the two preceding are on the state. It is our complimentary." He looks at the site of the explosion. "Certain things do not need to be mentioned," he says.

"I understand perfectly."

"A *good* day to you, sir. And thank you for all of your courtesies and understanding."

"You see?" Edna whispers as he skates off, "these are much better, much different than the old ones. They have kindness circuits built in for one thing."

"It's merely a different program."

"But they felt the *need* to make the program different," she says intensely. "Doesn't that tell you everything?"

"I don't know," I say, "I don't have your certainty."

"But the treatments aren't the answer. Faith comes from the inside."

"For some of us," I say. We stand together; our bodies collide. The touch, the slight incision we make against one another is stunning; I feel desire supersede dread. Edna takes my arm. "It wouldn't have been this way even a few years ago," she says, "we couldn't have had a public affectional; we couldn't have had the courage to love one another in front of the state."

"Perhaps," I say. "Perhaps." I am diffident. It is easier not to take a position in disagreement; besides Edna may well be right. Perhaps the state is benign; perhaps the treatments are a hoax, perhaps it is love and only love which under these auspices can save us. Hand in hand we walk through the cafe, barely seeing the sprawled bodies of the overanodyned, the affections clutching, the cooperatives staring past one another at walls the color of plasma. The servos part for us as we approach them; beam for identity and the absence of detonative devices, open the walls and let us through. In the corridor, brisk winds assail us coated with the smell of blood. The sounds of the undersystem, of the decompensates yielding their burden for the greater good.

"Quickly," Edna says, taking my elbow. "Quickly." She propels me through the corridors, murmuring words of pleasure. Enthralled by her, by love, by possibility, I follow.

"It will get better yet," she says as we approach the hydraulics which will take us to our cubicle. "You'll stop taking these foolish treatments, you'll understand that our destiny lies within our own hands and that we have the power to change, you'll give up on fanaticism and become a useful human being. The old man was taken away painlessly. Just a few years ago, who would have dreamed that we would have even this much?"

She is right. For the moment she is right. As they tell us, how could we have dreamed we would have even this much? The technicians have assured us of the improvements; who and why are we to dispute them?

Clutched by love, I wait for lovelies bleeding. The odors of slaughter are now flowers reaching, blooming in the night.

"The Father."
The Son. The Holy Ghost.

"Daniel."

The Lion's Den.

"Lot."

Pillar of Salt. Sodom. Gomorrah.

"Crucifixion."

Nails. Pain.

"Judas."

The Kiss.

The Confessor drops the sheet and looks at me with a sudden, open pleasure. "This is quite good," he says, "this is really remarkable. This is better than we would have imagined."

"Thank you," I say.

"Your grasp of the materials is quite stunning. It's surfaced above the preconscious."

"Indeed it has. I could have told you that."

"The question is what you're going to do with all of this knowledge once you have it."

I do not answer him. There is nothing to say. I could not, I dare not, I am far too sensible to, tell him the truth.

"I know what you're thinking," he says, "but it doesn't change the situation at all."

I stare at him. "It doesn't?"

"All of that is well accounted for," he says, "We do, after all, have history on our side."

He looks at the man who has come from the tomb. Little sign of entrapment is upon him; he looks merely as one might who had been in deep sleep for a couple of days. He touches him once gently upon the cheek to assure the pulse of light, then backs away. He is overcome. He is overcome by himself; he really was not sure that he could do this.

The crowd murmurs with awe. This is no small feat here; he has clearly outdone the loaves and the fishes. This one they will not be able to dismiss so quickly, it will cause profound comment when the news hits Rome. "How are you?" he says to Lazarus at a distance. "Have you merely been sleeping or did you perceive the darkness? Tell us; the question is important. What word have you brought back from those regions? Are they as we imagine or is there something beyond, a crest of light?"

Documentary sources, of course, indicate no speech from the risen Lazarus. But documentary sources are notoriously undependable and, in any case, this is a free reconstruction as he has been advised so often. He is making it up as he goes along out of his own history and inclination, he can do anything that he wants. Perhaps Lazarus will have something to say after all; his eyes bulge with reason and his tongue seems about to burst forward with the liquid syllables of discovery. "Come on, Lazarus," he says, "we're all attending. Tell us what it was like." Why not? Perhaps he will find out something which will enable him to deal with later antagonists. Assurances of any kind would be appreciated.

But Lazarus is only able to babble. Incoherent syllables rise, pass from his mouth. It is highly disappointing. The man seems stricken by fear or perhaps his brain is gone.

He moves in closer. "Were you sleeping?" he

says, "or did you perceive? This is very important to all of us and no one can give word but you."

"Ah," Lazarus says. "Eeeh. Om."

"What was that?"

"Ay. Om."

He shrugs and moves away. If a miracle is to work it must do so on its own terms, everyone knows this. One must have a detached, almost airy attitude toward the miracles because at the slightest hint of uncertainty or effort they will dissipate. "Very well," he says, "no more of this. You have been freed. Return to your life."

Lazarus, who does seem to understand, stares at him in consternation. What life indeed?

"Well," he says, "that's out of my hand. I created the loaves and fishes, I wasn't expected to eat them. I can't tell you exactly where to go after the tomb, now can I?"

Lazarus limps away, groaning quiet syllables. The disciples group around respectfully. Judas of course is missing; he is somewhere in the city no doubt making arrangements for betrayal as usual. There is little to be done about that; he must suffer Judas exactly as Judas must suffer him: it is the condition of their pact. Everything knits: Job and Satan too. The wondrous order of things is terrible in its density but there is beauty as well.

Peter puts a heavy hand on his shoulder. "What if the man is unable to care for himself, master?" he says, practical as always. "What if he is unable to complete the entire journey from the grave but remains in this condition? He will surely be friendless, he will starve and the miracle will be nullified."

"It will still be a miracle."

"Is that compassionate, master?"

Expect Peter to ask this question. "He will be able to care for himself," he says. "I would not perform a miracle of incompletion; he will be able to deal with himself. To have left him otherwise would be cruelty."

Indeed—even though he is inventing this on the spot; he had not expected this development or Peter's protest—Lazarus does seem to have adopted a stiff gait which takes him slowly toward the crowd and he is moving slowly but with purpose. The crowd is surprisingly sparse after all, hardly the throng indicated by the texts but instead might be only forty or fifty, many of whom are itinerants drawn to the scene through their wanderings. Scriptural sources are often only a foundation for the received knowledge, of course, the scribes had their own problems, their own needs to fill and retrospective falsification was part of the mission . . . still, he thinks it is often embarrassing to see how hollow that rock upon which the church was built. Oh well. Nothing can be taken at its word; there is manipulation and shading of the truth at every level. "He's doing fine," he says, observing some women patting Lazarus's limbs to be assured of their corporeality. "Don't worry; they'll care for him out of curiosity."

"In that case I think we'd better leave now," Peter says.

"Oh?"

"Indeed," this man of practicality says. "It will make more of an impression. Don't you think so, boys?"

The other disciples nod. Matthew makes a fist to show his seriousness. "Of course he's right," Matthew says. "Peter's always right. We should have listened to him from the beginning."

"It's a question of mystery," Peter says, "imparting a greater lasting effect than if you were to stay around. It might look as if you were soliciting their admiration whereas if you leave quickly it will show that you're beyond it. You have to cultivate a certain detachment to be taken seriously, to really succeed."

"We will surround you, Master," eager little Mark says, "and leave in a group, hiding your aspect from the populace. In this way you will seem to be attended at all times by a shield. A true prophet needs to be shielded; look at what happened to Jeremiah. You can't be in an exposed position."

The argument seems to have carried. Luke and John, Simon and Peter come forward. "Let's go," Peter says, giving instruction, "nothing can be served by staying here longer. It will be all to the best to move on."

He does admire the practicality here. The disciples are simply acting within the situation to maximize interest and to make of it legend as quickly as possible; they are surely working for him and yet a perverse reluctance tugs. He is really interested in Lazarus. Lazarus is fascinating. He would like to see what happens next, certainly the texts were not very functional on this point: will the man leave the area of the tomb or will he simply return to it? That is a possibility because the rock has merely been pulled aside, the dark opening gapes: Lazarus could simply return to that comfort if he desired. Perhaps he does. Perhaps he would like to skedaddle right back in there and embrace death once more, having found that it is a solution to his life problems. Or perhaps not; it is hard to evaluate the responses of an individual who has come from the tomb and essayed an affecting but crippled gait. The man is in any case now shielded from view by the crowd which seems to be touching him, checking for the more obvious evidences of mortality. "Let's wait a moment here," he says, "this is very interesting. Let's see what's going to happen here."

"No, Master," Mark says. "Peter feels that it will not be right and we should listen to him."

"Peter is working for *me*. Besides, you can write all of this down along with the other parts. Don't you want to know how it turned out?"

"Not for the sake of an unfortunate miracle."

"It would not serve, Master," Peter says determinedly. "It would not serve at all; it would smack of vanity. If we do not leave now the moment will be lost and it will not matter whether we stay or not. We must seize it."

"I'd just like to *observe*," he says. "Is there anything wrong with curiosity? It may be ignoble but it is not harmful and it is the bridesmaid of result. I *am* responsible for this Lazarus after all; it is only reasonable that I would take an interest in his condition after the tomb. After all," I say portentously, "it might apply to me, someday."

"No," Luke says. He scuttles over, a thin man with bulging, curiously piercing eyes. No wonder he wrote the most elaborate of the Gospels—dictated that is to say. All of the disciples are fundamentally illiterate; most of the population here cannot deduce even the most basic symbols. "It is important that we leave at once, Master; there can be no further delay."

"Why? I'm the leader of this group, I can do anything that I want to do." A whining, somewhat petulant tone has overtaken; I am somewhat surprised at my own manner. One can see where under certain circumstances I could be an irritating man. "I can stay as long as I please, until I please."

"No," Luke says firmly. "The mood of this crowd is uncertain; it could turn ugly at any time. There has been a great deal of argument over these miracles and superstition can turn quickly to fear. The very hills are filled with great portents, the heavy sound of wings beating—"

"Enough," Peter says. "Enough. You have a tendency for hyperbole, Luke, there is no danger here that I can see but merely a loss of credibility. It would be better from many standpoints if we were to leave, a certain air of mystery would serve best—"

"Oh all right," I say, somewhat petulantly. I am weary of the circularity of the discussion; if this is the way that business was conducted amidst the disciples it is indeed remarkable that anything got done, let alone the many flourishes and divinities which have gained my posthumous reputation. "Je renounce. I renunciate this." It is, after all, best to adopt a pose of dignity and to give into the disciples' wishes. All of them take these matters far more seriously than I it would seem . . . if they are creations of my own unconscious, they are serious creations whereas I am a frivolous one; then too, according to all of the texts their situation is certainly a far more exposed one than mine . . . I will be out of this and they will have to deal with the consequences, the populace. Paul and Timothy reach out their hands and assist me from the site. I cast one final look back at Lazarus who is now leaning against the suspended door of the tomb, elbows balanced precariously on stones, trying to assume an easeful posture for the group which almost obscures him. He seems to be carrying all of this off very well although I cannot hear a word that he is saying, doubtless he is still babbling in tongues; whatever it is, however, it seems persuasive.

How exactly is one to cultivate a je ne sais quoi about death? This will be my own problem soon enough; it is worth considering but Lazarus, I deduce could hardly yield much information on the subject. If I am looking for someone to advise me he does not appear to be the proper source. The man is speechless, highly inarticulate; one would have hoped that for a miracle such as this I could have aroused someone less stupid but nothing to be done. All of existence is a parade of the creatures, linked head by tail in a single tapestry, take it all or leave it: no divisions, no parts. The famous and the dead. Surrounded by my muttering disciples I walk toward the west, kicking up little stones and puffs of dust with my sandals.

Disappointing. It is quite a letdown to be sure

and I would like to discuss this but there is not a one of them who would want to hear it or could understand what I was saying. I know that this bunch already have their problems, having elected to give up their lives for mine for the duration of this mission and it would be an embarrassment to suggest to them that I too do not quite know what I am doing.

Or perhaps I do. Perhaps I know exactly what I am doing and this stumbling, bumbling, self-loathing journey in the Gospels will have assumed the retrospective burnishment and fire of the purest and most mystical purpose. This is possible. All things are possible. It is hard to tell. One should not make easy judgements. One should be slow to rise, slow to fail. Early in the bed and early to rise. Hear the cock crow.

In the distance I hear the vague collision of stone. I would not be surprised if Lazarus, having had a good look at the way and condition of the world had not decided to flee back to the tomb. One could hardly blame him for this. Of the tapestry of his own existence I have no idea. Of the tapestry of mine I can see pattern. Je ne sais pais. Je ne sais pas and the cracked bottles for the old wine lie safe and waiting in the vault.

At Passover a large and companionable gathering. Judas leans over me for an instant and advises that he will have to leave early; he has important business in town concerned with smoothing my way with the populace but he will be sure to return by midnight. He is so transparent that it is amusing; I want to point out to him that there is no reason for him to show such anxiety about his connivance; no less than me he is merely trying to perform a role and be done with this. "It's all right, old fellow," I say, clasping his hand, "don't worry about it, I trust you implicitly. Stay out all night if you wish."

His hand squirms in my clutch, his eyes shift desperately. "That won't be necessary," he says, "just a little bit of business, I'll hardly be missed, I'll be back before you know it." The man is in pain sufficient to his burden. "I promise," he mutters, "I promise," and withdraws, Peter takes his place, pours a glass of wine and devours it with a flourish.

"I think things are going very well," he says, "excellently in fact. Riding in on a donkey was a masterful stroke; I'm glad that you listened to us on that. And coming immediately here, away from the crowds was wonderful; there's quite an air of excitement and mystery. I told you, didn't I, that this would be the best way to stir up interest?"

"Don't worry about it, Peter," I say, "before the cock crows you too will have denied me three times."

He looks startled. "What's that?" he says, "I don't understand."

"Not to worry," I say, "nothing personal. Not your fault." I am in a merry state. Part of it is the wine of course; part comes from knowing that soon this will be over. There are only a few more tasks which will order themselves out and then I will be ready for completion. In the meantime there is nothing wrong with getting drunk and having a good time. I pour myself another glassful and drink it heartily. Peter raises a cautionary hand but I brush it away. "Don't worry," I say, "go back to your seat. Everything's fine; you don't have to give orders all the time."

"I'm not giving orders, just trying to make things work a little more smoothly."

"Things are going very smoothly," I say loudly, "they could not be better!" the wine brings a flush to my cheek, clap to my hand and Peter staggers back from the table. Surrounded by glasses, disciples, food and my sense of mission I eat and drink my way methodically. Now and then soldiers detailed to observe us peek in through tent flaps; I nod cheerfully, brandish a bottle of wine, gesture them in but they drop the flaps and withdraw. Isolated for so long in the desert and then with the disciples, a goodhearted but essentially dull group, I would welcome new company but the soldiers refuse to enter, doubtless on orders from Pilate who will have other employment for them shortly. I am grateful to see that I am not the only one at table drunk, Mark and Timothy in particular have abandoned their seats entirely and sit on the ground, clashing glasses, laughing and whispering to one another. Enough of the wilderness is enough; I might have lasted longer with Satan if I had had some respite in the middle of those forty days and forty nights.

"Where is Judas Iscariot?" Peter says to me. I can see him only hazily; his bland features seem diffuse and extended to enormous proportion. "I haven't seen him for hours."

"Off on business. Don't worry about him."

"What business?"

"He's off with the Romans betraying me for thirty pieces of silver," I say merrily, "don't let it concern you."

Peter's mouth stretches; his eyes seem to overtake his forehead. "What are you telling me?"

"Nothing to worry about. Merely fulfillment of the sacred texts. Each of us has a job to do and each of us I must say is doing it quite well. Which reminds me, isn't it time for you to start denying me, Peter? Cock crow is hours off but nonetheless—"

He drags me to my feet. "Master," he says, "you are drunk. No more of this. You must go to bed."

"I'll go to bed when I want to," I say. I pull his hands off me. "No one is going to interfere with me when at last I'm having a good time."

"Master, for your own protection—"

"I said no one," I say loudly and back away from him, lose my balance, fight for purchase, cannot find it and pitch headlong onto the table upsetting bottles of wine, sending foodstuffs spinning. It is time for another set-to of loaves and fishes but I seem quite unable to get any control of the situation; I feel them seize me by the heels and flapping like a blanket I am taken from the table.

This strikes me for some reason as funny and I giggle lightly as they convey me toward the darkness. They said that I would come in *riding* upon an ass but not necessarily that I would be one. Upon such distinctions that rock could founder.

"You're sick, Master, you need sleep," I hear Peter say and this is about all that I hear for a long time. As I drift into the wide tunnels of unconsciousness it begins to occur to me why all the stations of the cross might have seemed as widely separated, as powerfully disorienting as they were.

As I copulate with Edna, my greatest and final affectional, images of martyrdom tumble through my mind: a stricken figure pinned on wood, stigmata ripped like lightning through the exposed sky, the chantings and pleas of the faithful as slowly, for their sake, I expire. It is all that I can do under the circumstances to perform; martyrdom has never for me been sexually exciting but they will be done our Father who art; I giveth this day her daily bread, the will transcends, forgiving, even assisting all of my trespasses and so I force myself into that unchallenged place of her, squeezing out the images, forgive me as I forgive you who trespass against me, her whimpers like birdshot through me for thine is the kingdom as she coils and uncoils like a springed steel object and the power and at long last sexual release, glory, glory: I do so myself by reflex and then fall from her grunting. It is all quite mechanical, this must be admitted but in a highly technologized culture sexual union could only be such: otherwise it would be quite threatening to the apparatus of the state. Or so at least I have deduced. The first power which the state would seek would be that to control relationships, to manage union.

Edna lies beside me, her face closed to all feeling, her fingers clawed around my wrist. I groan deeply and compose for sleep. Necessity is for necessity's sake but there are things which must be done in the morning: I need my rest.

But there is no sleep. She moves against me, hands clambering on my limbs and then sits upright in the bed, staring. Aspect of confrontation: elbows jutting at an angle of eighty-five degrees. I regard her bleakly.

"It's no good," she says, "Harold, it's no good at all; can't you see that it's not working?"

Questions of utility have replaced those of emotion at all levels of the culture; that is one of the reasons I sought the hypnotics. "I don't want to talk now," I say. "Please, if you must say something let it be later; there's nothing right now, nothing at all and it's late, Edna."

"You mean you have to face your damned treatments in the morning."

"Maybe that is what I mean."

"You need your rest so that you can be alert when they pump the theater into your system. That's all you think about now, those treatments. Where are you living? Here or there? Come on, tell me what really matters?"

"I don't want to talk," I say patiently, "Edna, I don't want to talk at all, I just want to rest. This is not the time to go into a discussion of the treatments—"

"You've changed," she says flatly, "they've destroyed you. You aren't what you used to be at all; I can't even recognize you sometimes any more."

There comes a time in every relationship when

one has approached terminus, when the expenditure of pain is not worth the input of pleasure, where one can feel the raw edges of difference collide through the dissolved flesh of care. Looking at Edna I see that we have reached that point, that there is not much left and that it will be impossible for me to see her again. This must be the end for its own sake.

She will leave and there will be no recurrence; what is happening in this room now is final. It is this certainty more than anything else which enables me to turn from her with equanimity, to confront the bold and staring face of the wall which looks upon me with more knowledge and compassion than Edna could ever find again.

"Goodnight," I say, "we will not talk about any of this any more. It is finished."

"You can't avoid it."

"I can avoid anything."

"You can run from me but not from what has happened. You're not *living* here any more; you're living in the spaces of your own consciousness. Don't you know that? You've turned inside, you've shut out everything. These aren't experiences that you're having, Harold, they are dreams and all of this is taking place inside you. I hate to see it happen; you're better than this, together we could have helped one another, worked to understand what our lives were, made a kind of progress. Remember the cafe—"

"The cafe was a lie, Edna."

She stares at me. "A lie?"

"An old man was trapdoored; a robot exploded.

Nothing is working any more; below the surface are the fires."

"But it doesn't have to be that way. It's possible to change the fires, save the old men—"

"Nothing is going to save the old men. *We* are the old men, Edna, and bit by bit, piece by piece they will burn us out so that there is nothing." I stand, shaking in the dim light. "I think you should leave now."

Arms folded across her little breasts, she glares at me. "That won't solve anything at all," she says. "Nothing. Getting rid of me will change nothing."

"I'm not getting rid of you. Old men are gotten rid of. I'm just asking you to leave."

"You'll still be here and you'll still be lying."

"The only truth," I say, "is the truth that we create within ourselves."

"I don't believe that. I never did. That's what they tell us, that's still what the technicians would have us believe, that's what got you started on the hypnotics and the treatments but it isn't so. There's an objective truth and it is outside of this and you're going to have to face it. You can't stay under the hypnotics forever; you're going to have to deal with this. You're going to have to realize—"

"Realize what?"

"Realize the nature of the life that we're living; realize the fact of the state and that things can change, they can be improved, they *are* going to get better but only because of the efforts of those who work with it in reality, who meet it on the proper terms, not by dreaming their lives away. Things must be changed—"

I look at her with enormous dispassion and my expression must be a blade which falls heavily across her rhetoric, chopping it. Silencing her. Her eyes become credulous, enormous and round they stare at me. I listen to the passage of her breath, confront her in the spaces of the room bringing to bear upon her all the force which I have acquired, all of the insights and at length she is not only silent but open, her head tilted at an acute angle, a child's head inclined to receive messages or gifts.

And it is only then that I give her the necessary question. I pose it as flatly and calmly as I have ever done and its resonance fills the room, my heart, her eyes, until there is nothing else ahead of us but her flight and after that the peace which I have promised myself, the pure crosswinds all mine alone, tilting the soul.

"Why?" I say.

Her mouth opens but she is incapable of speech.

"Why?"

"Don't take it so personally," I say to the Magdalene. I give her an encouraging nudge in the ribs, against her will she begins to smile. "It doesn't matter what you were; all that concerns us is what you will become, eh?" She is a shy girl, overwhelmed by circumstances and not responsive to the aspect of crowds or demonstrations which means that she is hardly suited for this life. On the other hand she is devoted to me in a gentle, unthreatening fashion and this too is what I need; the fervor of some of the disciples, the skepticism of the crowds are not a milieu in which one can find any peace. "Come on," I say, "it isn't that difficult? Things are getting better all the time; look what you've learned."

She looks at me shyly under the tree where we have paused in the endless walk toward Rome. "It's not that I haven't learned, Master," she says, "it's what they must think of me."

"Who thinks what of you?"

"The others. Your disciples. I've heard them talking about me, whispering behind their hands. They don't think well of me and they're ashamed. They don't think I should be here at all."

"That's preposterous," I say although it is not; I have had some lively discussions with Peter on exactly this point. "Let him who is without sin and so forth. All of us are fallible here."

"Nonetheless," she says, "nonetheless." She tilts up the ewer of water, takes a delicate swallow. There is an intensity in her eyes, a fixation in that stare which makes me uneasy and suddenly I do not want to continue the conversation. "We have a long way to go," I say, "we cannot tarry for a while."

"Why do you want me along, Master?"

"It is you who wants to be here."

"Yes, but why do you tolerate me? Why do you stand for me against all the others?"

It is a difficult question but I am not equipped to deal with it at this time. Perhaps not at all. Perhaps never. "Because you want to be here," I say, "that is sufficient." Standing with her in this way I am aware of the heat, the intensity of the desert, the stares of the others as they watch us from a safe distance. "Come on," I say, taking her hand, "we might as well be going."

Her clutch against me is scaled by the heat yet moistens to a kind of tenderness. "You'll never know," Mary says, "you'll never know what this means to me."

"I have made the loaves and the fishes; I have wrestled with Satan in the desert and you tell me that I'll never know?"

She laughs at me in a strange and knowledgeable way, takes my other hand, holds them clasped below her waist. "No," she says, "Jesus, you'll never know."

Aaron rushes to assist me as I stagger the last steps, struggling with the enormous blocks of stone. They cascade from my hands and I fall before him, grunting, in a moment they are all around me, bending forward, touching me, but Aaron screams, "Leave him alone, leave him alone now!" and they move away. The crevices in the stones are illegible this close; within those spaces I can see only the blood which came from my palms as I carried them. "Are you all right?" Aaron says. He wipes my brow, takes my pulse.

"I will never live to get out of this desert," I say.

"You? You will *lead* us out of this desert."

"I will lead you but I will never get out of it myself. So it is destined."

"Did you learn that on the mountain?" he says.

"Oh no," I say, "oh no, no, no, I was summoned to the mountain to transcribe and I did that very well. I found that out all myself on the way down."

"How?"

"It occurred to me," I say. "It occurred to me that a God who would send us through all of these years in the emptiness, who would exchange one form of slaughter for another and whose gift for all of this time would be the provision of powerful and restrictive sanction, a God who would take note of our suffering while putting little but proscription into our hands . . . such a God would not allow me out of the desert but would in final vindication make my death a cause of passage."

Aaron stares, says nothing. Whether or not he agrees with me he has always shown respect. "That is true," I say, "and that is just one of many truths."

"We will have no passage without you," Aaron says, "no true passage can be accomplished."

"That is right," I agree, "and that is also what I learned as I carried the stones. Because in the most profound and terrible way all of us have been sentenced to live on the desert forever."

"Forever?"

"Forever and ever," I say quietly.

At Bruck Linn they do not start the pogrom after all. My reading of the situation was wrong; they are going along with the bans. Terror matters, threats are always effective but lives are spared; my penitents and supplicants are scattered by their boots like screaming chickens as I am seized and hurled into detention. The manner of their coming was merely to threaten and divert; they came in such numbers only to make sure that the area could be scoured if I were not at my appointed place.

Detention is a set of basement rooms in an enormous building across the waters that at one time had functioned as a kind of municipal center; now it is arrayed with pictures of the founders and antique, decommissioned torture devices but bears little administrative function. The quarters are no worse than what I have been accustomed to for most of my professional life.

In detention I find beds, tables, cabinets, holy texts, writings, dishes, storage boxes and the five sacred books of the Pentauch which, since they take me to be a religious man are their own special gift to the premises. Apparently they have no plans to kill me quickly; the presence of the books is re-assuring. Then again they merely may be suggest-ing that I squeeze in some hasty reading before I am executed. In either case, I look through them idly, munching on a piece of stale cake which they have left on the table but as always I find the dead and sterile phrases insufficient on their own terms to provoke reaction. It is hard to intermingle with the sacred texts; although I am a man of learning I have never found much satisfaction in the books, preferring rather to test myself on the field of hu-man endeavor and interchange. Talmudic disputa-tion interests me but only as a function of person-ality; as a means of gaining advantage.

It is with relief then that I see them come into my room early on the third day of my confinement. Obviously they are there to explain themselves and to explain their program; it is high time. Both are splendidly uniformed but one apparently is relegated to the role of secretary; without acknowledging me he sets up a recording device in the corner of the room and sits, donning earphones. The other, a little older, has a blunt face and surprisingly expressive eyes; I would not have thought that they would be permitted large wet blue eyes such as this. It is a contradiction in the terms that I have assigned but then again it might only be an example of their cunning.

"Rabbi," he says directly, sitting across from me, "you are giving us much difficulty. Too much by far and so we have had to arrange this rather difficult interview."

"It is not difficult so far," I say wisely, attempting to keep them off balance. It is best not to be predictable as this forces them to move out of their range; the same rules apply to *pilpul*. "So far this interview has been very easy."

"This interview has not yet begun."

"It began when you entered."

He pauses, then sighs in controlled irritation. "I was warned not to get into argument with you," he says, "and so I will not. Our apologies for the melodrama but it could not, you must know, be spared. We needed to seize and detain as quickly as possible."

"That you did."

"We could not run the risk of riots, of protests."

"My followers are devoted but they are cowards," I say, "those who engage in logical or religious disputation are not what you would call Maccabees."

"We did not know."

"On the other hand I am a world figure. My abduction in your mind could hardly have been expected to be this easy. You had to plan for the worst."

"It's not only that," he says, "it's not quite what you think."

"But that in itself—my stature, my reputation—would be enough."

"Possibly. No matter anyway, it falls outside this." He looks at me intently. "We're going to have to abort the treatments," he says. "You're becoming obsessive."

This statement utterly falls out of my experience; I do not know how to deal with it. I stare at him. "What are you talking about? What treatments?"

He looks at me carefully, his eyes narrowing in concentration. "I believe you," he says, "I believe what you are saying; that you do not understand who I am or what I mean. This is very sad and disturbing although not quite unprecedented."

"I don't know what you're talking about," I say astonished, "I have no understanding of this at all. What are you trying to tell me? What is this about?"

"The treatments have obviously leached into your personal life; you are beginning to blend them and objective reality in a dangerous fashion because you will soon lose the ability to segregate the hypnotic process from the mundane details of your life and will become psychotic. Therefore—"

"Hypnotics? Process?"

"Therefore, under the contract we are exercising

the option which was signed. We are going to cut them off before serious damage is risked."

"I have no understanding of this," I say, "Treatments? Hypnotics? Objective reality? I am the Lubavitcher Rabbi of Bruck Linn in the city of Queens and I have been torn from the heart of my congregation in open daylight by fascists. I have been shamed in front of my followers, a terrible judgement has been brought upon me, one which will affect the validity of all circumstances, which will call into question my ability to counsel them at all times heretofore. That is what you have done to me and now you speak of hypnotics and counsel." My hands shake, I take a slab of bread, tear it apart, begin to chew upon it maniacally to try to ease the trembling. It is almost hopeless but I must somehow retain my dignity. Dignity is all that is left, without that I have nothing. "This is unspeakable," I say, unfurling one of the linens they have given me and expectorating into it. "Absolutely unspeakable. You are counselling madness."

He takes the bread from my hands, removes a small piece of it himself and flicks away the seeds, then drops it to the ground. "I am afraid," he says and those expressive eyes are linked to mine, "that you are displaying precisely those symptoms which have made this necessary. You are not the Lubavitcher Rabbi, let alone of Bruck Linn in the city of Queens. You have imagined all of this outside the program; you have created it yourself, you are Harold Thwaite of the twenty-third century in Denmark."

"Denmark? A brave Jewish community there, they were protected by the king—"

"There have been no Jews in Denmark for decades. There are no Jews anywhere in the world. The Lubavitchers are a defunct, forgotten sect and you are imagining all of this. You have reconceived your life, the partitions have broken, you are bleeding through all the cubicles and compartments of your life and we are therefore for your own protection ceasing the treatments and placing you in temporary detention."

"I am in prison, that is where I am."

"You imagine these facilities, Harold, you are actually in our custody in the center. You will be all right, everything will be manageable, you will be taken from this condition and bit by bit, piece by piece your life will be reassembled. We are not out to destroy personalities here but to integrate them and for the sake of your integration every means will be adopted." He takes the bread from my hand. "You will be placed on a special diet. Intravenous feeding may be indicated for a while as you clear the formula from your system."

"What is this?" I say. "Formulae? Systems? Is this alchemy?"

"It is technology. Which in your case has been somewhat misapplied but everything will be worked out for the best."

"This is a pogrom," I say, "and a pogrom I can understand. But with such sophistry? Advanced with such deceit? This I do not think that I can handle; this is madness beyond me. None of the Nazis were as mad as you."

The uniformed man leans toward me and with the gentlest of fingers strokes my cheek. "It will go easier if you cooperate, Harold," he says. "I know how difficult this must be for you, the shock, the unseating of circumstance, the intrusion which we have made. I must be reminded to see it from your perspective and from that perspective it looks very threatening. But everything will be all right; you are in capable and competent hands."

"My followers will avenge me."

"Harold," the man says, "you have no followers."

"They will *avenge* me. You will not find them easy to deal with; you will have to cut them down with rifle fire, pile their corpses high as you did in Germany. You have the machinery and power to do this; I will not deny that, you can apply all of the great engines to our destruction but the cost in blood and bodies will be high, very high and in the long run you cannot win."

"Harold—"

"You cannot *win,* every corpse is testimony, every mute child witness, every exterminated soul a bird free to scream at the temples. In the focus of eternity we will prevail because everything is weighed, all of it is weighed and understood. *We* are God's chosen, the scepter of humanity and of us only the Lubavitchers carry forth the living presence in this century and you cannot tamper with that presence unless you are willing human sacrifice, unless you are willing to accept not only the destruction of the temple but the destruction of the self. From on high I call malediction—".

I stop.

I become aware of his aspect.

And I see to my amazement and to my dismay that the interrogator, the one who has come to intimidate and defile, this man in the hard and terrible uniform of the state, is weeping.

In the beginning the affections are assigned but later on choice becomes operative. After some experience with love and pain we are granted more or less to do with it as we wish. Even then we must choose affections in the same Cluster, affectionals whose life experience and choices roughly parallel ours. This they say is for the sake of the relationship but the truth is that from disparity might come passions of the ugliest sort, passions which would so absorb us that we would come to neglect their power.

Edna's hands are light on mine as we meet for our preliminary public encounter. At change of shift the sweepers are throughout the enclosure, replacing tufts of grass, straightening flowers, restocking the aviaries but enmeshed in one another we pay this only the slightest attention. Technology need not be the enemy of desire but can move to quicken; it is only a matter of attitude. Her cheekbones show the suggestion of torment, her eyes indicate damage, her lovely neck, inclined to look at me as I hold her hands, kneel at her feet shows that it has been tested by weeping; many of her affectionals, I suspect, have ended badly and no more than I is she at home in this century. Nonetheless we will not discuss backgrounds for a long time; it is understood that preliminary affections must concentrate on the unfolding instant. "It's too warm here," Edna says, "they should take the climate down."

"Some of the birds need heat." Around us other preliminary affectionals are scattered on the grass, some are talking at a distance but others, verifying the efficacy of the selection process are already copulating enthusiastically. Modestly I turn my gaze from them; I would not want to share their circumstance any more than I would want them to share mine. "I have lived here for three years," I say, "I am promised larger quarters. I used to work at the institute but now I am on relief. There is the possibility of an inheritance. I do not really know what to make of or what to do with my life. Everything seems very uncertain. Less and less do I feel in control of it and yet I do not want to seize control because I would make it even worse. Do you know what I mean?"

"Yes," she says. "I studied the harp but found that there were no places for the instrument in this Cluster and I did not want to move. I have lived here all of my life. My forebears are deceased. Now and then I think that it could be different than this but I am not sure exactly why or how. I have a diseased, romantic sensibility, my last affectional told me. I know we are not supposed to talk of that but he wouldn't leave the subject alone. You impute meanings where there are none, he said. Why can't you simply accept this on its own terms and deal with it? But I think that things can change and be better. Don't you agree? Sometimes I think that even in a few short years matters have changed."

"I'm not sure," I say, "the state seems immovable. Perhaps we can change but the state never."

"We live within the state; if it does not change then all of our own efforts to do so are delusion. You have a nice mouth," Edna says. She puts a finger on the corner of a lip, slowly strokes it. "You show more sensitivity in your mouth than I think you have in your soul. Let me test it and find out. I cannot kiss your soul but I can trust your mouth." She leans, plants a cool pressure against mine; slowly it unwinds into an enclosure full of rope and odors from dark objects hidden in the damp. Her tongue seems to clatter against my teeth, then slowly withdraws. "There," she says, "that wasn't bad, was it? That wasn't so bad at all."

"I didn't say it was."

"You're afraid to kiss. Something within you holds back; you may be afraid of the vulnerability." Her hand runs across my knee. "You need your affectionals yet are afraid of them. If you had to find them on your own, you might have found none at all. In your case the state has been a patron." Her fingers trace a pattern. "Don't you think?"

"Some of my affectionals have been meaningful."

"I'm sure that they have. But that was not the question I was asking. How many of them would you have found on your own?"

"I don't know," I say. "A few. Three. Possibly

two. It does not matter." A nest of mechanical birds topples from the roof of an aviary and falls to the sod, I look at them with dull sympathy. I suspect that I know how it would feel to be an artificial bird stunningly deposed. "What matters is not procuration but dynamic, don't you think?"

"You have a strange way of talking. I've never known anyone who uses words the way you do. Do you want to try another kiss?"

I lean forward, feel that tentative touch opening once again into a powerful and draining sustenance. One could become obsessed by kissing; I see this as if for the first time. She gasps, pours air into my throat, I feel myself swell with every exhalation. When we break it is as if I am a different person and nothing that happens to me from here on will ever be the same once more.

"You see?" she says, "you're not so experienced. There's a lot you have to learn."

"I know," I say, "I have plans. I don't want to live like this forever. There must be something else, something beyond the state, some means of perception—"

She looks quickly around her. "You sound like a revolutionary."

"I'm not a revolutionary. I only want to take life seriously."

"So how will you do that?"

"I don't want to talk about that yet," I say, "this is not the time. There will be other moments, a process perhaps—"

She shrugs. "I don't want to hear about it any more. So do you want to sign a contract?"

"You asked me to tell you about my plans," I say, "and when I began to talk you said you didn't want to hear any more." I look at her little face, the faint dimpling of one cheekbone and for the first time see deep within to some sense of the woman, some human inconstancy which speaks to my condition in a way she has not before. "I don't understand."

"Don't ask me to be consistent," she says. She smiles in a private way as if she had glimpsed herself in my perception. "Consistency leads to obliteration."

"I want to sign a contract," I say.

She looks at me, her face open and alight, her hands rising to touch my face. "I'm glad," she says and opens her mouth, I find myself being drawn once again toward that sliding and tunnelled connection through which—as I feel her lips touch mine—I now know that I seek myself. "Oh God," she murmurs as the kiss at last is broken, "oh God, every time the same but everytime difference; in the difference is the infinite replication," and slowly, slowly we tumble from the bench, fall to the twisted and mechanical grass, fall amidst all of the other affections clutching and there no less than the others or the false birds, the dead and rumbling animals of the memorial zoo we celebrate in our way the tender and awful devices of the century. Plunging, rising. Clutching, holding. Retracting, devouring.

Known and known yet again.

I part the Red Sea with a flourish of the cane.

The waters furl like pennants caught by the wind and the dry bed is exposed, astonished sharks and lesser fishes gasp and flap on the damp, open sands. Behind me there are astonished murmurs. I gesture. "This is our way of passage," I say. "Let us take it and cross before the troops are here. This is the means of our deliverance."

I step aside so that they may cross, the young and old, hearty and ill, suspicious and devoted but they do not move. They stare at me with wondering gaze. "Now?" I say and gesture with the cane once more. They do not move. I turn to Aaron, faithful as always by my side. "What is going on here?" I say, "why don't you think that they'll cross?"

"Why don't you ask them?"

"I'm asking you."

"I'll ask them," Aaron says. He moves among them quickly, bending, hovering, consulting, taking testimony. He has always been the intermediary; if they are awed by me Aaron has been the more linking presence. Perhaps they have always felt me to be a bit crazy although I am their acknowledged leader. Aaron kneels, talks to a saintly, patriarchal type who is joined by several women, they whisper to him frantically, he listens, nods, stands convulsively and then comes back toward me. I hold the cane like a prayer book. "I'm afraid they don't trust the evidence," Aaron says to me.

"What?"

"That seems to be the consensus here. They've never seen seas part before, they're not sure that it might not be a mirage. This is not a sophisticated bunch, you know, they're a bunch of slaves and peasants."

"But *I* didn't perform the parting? You know who did."

"Oh *I* know who did," Aaron says agreeably, "but I've pointed out that this is by and large an ignorant bunch. They're not as convinced of the existence of your God as I am."

"That's blasphemous!"

"It may be, Moses, but why would any God perform miracles for a bunch of slaves. That seems to be the consensus that I've picked up, anyway. Oh, and they also are afraid that even if it isn't a mirage, it may be a trap of some kind. As soon as they really get into the sea the waters may close upon them."

"Why would anything like that happen?"

"Call it a persecution complex," Aaron says wisely, "there is after all some reason for this on the record."

I grip the cane, feeling the recrimination and fury build. "That's ridiculous," I say, "would I take them this far, do so much, get them out of Egypt, confer on the plagues, visit such ruin upon the House of the King only to betray them at this time? Would any God that had taken them this far undo them?"

Aaron shrugs, a bucolic, pleasant sort, given to bumbling but quite realistic in many ways, more in tune with the people, the tenor of the times than I in many ways I admit. "What can I tell you?" he says resignedly, "there's no accounting for interpretation. It's a highly subjective business."

* * *

"Oh, I wouldn't worry about it," my elderly Comforter says, "marital stress is very common under circumstances like this; wives that can be perfectly agreeable as long as things are going well can become bitches under stress; marriages that could survive indefinitely as long as the cattle are healthy and gold is in the stockhouse go askew when misfortune strikes and it's no one's fault, not yours, certainly not your wife's." He laughs suddenly, takes a long drink of wine, stares at me. "Those boils are disgusting," he says, "have you been picking them?"

"Not that I know."

"You can risk terrible infections but then again," the elderly Comforter says, hoisting the wine bottle, "then again in your situation I must say that I'd probably do anything to keep my mind off my troubles right to boil-picking." He squints, shades his eyes, looks out at the fields. "My oh my," he says, "you sure have a bunch of dead cattle there, Job. I wouldn't want to be in your situation at all. And then again," he says, tilting the bottle of wine, looking at the sediment, then raising it to his lips, "then again, I'm *not* am I? The way I figure is you brought it all on yourself, anyway."

The bullet hits my temple.

The impact is devastating; I fall, my blood leaping ahead of me to the floor and yet I am still able to think. The cerebellum has been destroyed but I seem to retain the ability to think and it is this and the pain which makes things even worse. *They were more serious than I,* I realize. Compared to them I was frivolous because I was willing to trust the outcome of my rebellion to a higher power whereas they, sober and solemn businessmen, decided to make sure that the matter rested in their own hands; that if losses overbalanced profits they would seek a solution. I was the fool who thought that what was begun in transcendence would continue there; that divinity and its considerations would overtake all.

O my oh my o Lord it *hurts.* The skull opens, the slow brains ooze forth, the pulped and empty fruit of the sensibility begins to spread through the widening crack; I see the ripe and decaying matter of the brain. And who would have known, who would have known that there was so much pain in it until they put me down at the mosque, put me down at the heart of my purpose and o God o God tell them Malcolm now and tell them true, tell them from the high mountains and from all the temples of Judea, go tell it from the mountaintop and in all the cities of the Lord that no passion no passion no passion is worthy of this blood streaming, this blood darkness, this blood-rent pain as I fall and fall and fall and o my Lord the screaming the screaming and the fear.

"Face the truth," the serpent says, "you enjoy the chaos, the endless division, the schism and the struggle; if you didn't you wouldn't have dismissed me to walk to and fro upon the earth and up and down upon it. You got bored with the void, the amorphous darkness; that wasn't enough for you."

Old tempter. Even I am not immune to his devices and this makes me feel less vengeful toward the wretched people who I have exiled from Eden. If I cannot be unshaken by him, what chance did they have when he appeared smiling with the perfect fruit? Millennia pass while I ponder his statement. Eons creak by while I give it further thought. The anguish of the centuries passes as if in a blink while I give it true and proper consideration. "You do not understand any of this. It is beyond your means to cope so I will not argue with you."

"If it is beyond my means," the serpent says, "then that too is your responsibility because no less than the others I am your creation, don't you understand that? You exiled me to do this; if I have done it in a certain way that too was your decision. *You have replicated all of this out of yourself.* The universe is your responsibility and you must seek it."

It is a cunning argument, filled with passion and lore, filled with the ugly and accumulated wisdom of all the millennia which I have let flick past and yet I cannot permit it to move me because the serpent is by definition evil and this is the counsel of darkness. So I say nothing and I say nothing and I say nothing, pondering what I can do to at last demonstrate the imperfect and struggling condition of my will while he rolls on his belly and smiles, chews dry fruit and smiles, whispers my name deep in his throat and counsels his own vengeance.

At last and at length through more of this,

through more introspection than is even proper, perhaps, for one with my powers, I have a perception and the perception leads to an insight. "I will prove you wrong," I say, "I will show you that you deceive." I roll in the heavens and regard him.

"It cannot be done."

"There is a way and this way is this," I say, "I will send my perfect and only begotten son to these burnt and awful places and I will show you what happens to him, the truest expression of my will."

The serpent nibbles on a stalk of grass. "It is a foolishness," he says, "it will prove nothing."

"No," I say, "and conversely it will prove everything. If my will is replicate then one thing will happen but if it is not as I will prove then it is another."

"Oh my," says the serpent, "oh my, oh my, why don't you simply spare both of us and get on directly to Revelations and be done with it? Wouldn't that be easier?"

"Nothing was meant to be easy."

"With that," the serpent says, "I can agree."

"Do you see now?" the Counselor says. "Do you understand the situation? You are clearly in need of help." His hands flutter, a glare of consternation passes through his features, he grips his desk as if he were about to fall beneath it. "There is no shame in this I want to emphasize," he says, "and a great deal of precedent for the circumstance."

"Nothing has ever been like this," I tell him. "There has never been anything like this in all history. I am on the verge of a true and terrible insight."

"They all feel that way. It is one of the symptoms: grandiosity. All of you who get this way feel that you're exceptional but that just isn't so. It's an overload, an inability of the circulatory system to flush, that's all, it can be controlled in routine ways, a period of phased withdrawal—"

"There is no phased withdrawal from life," I say wisely, "you're either in it or out of it. Similarly from the heavens or the bowels of the earth. There are no intermediaries, there is merely a fullness." He darts in and out of the center of vision. "For a certainty," I say.

"We know how to treat this; it is very precise. All that we require is a minimum cooperation, a certain trust and humility and you will be on your way before very long at all."

"I am humble," I say. "Oh my yes, I am humble. Humility is not the problem."

"The fact that you are back in focus now for instance is a very promising sign. Just a few hours ago we thought that we might lose you, that you had slipped completely under the hypnotics and that we would have to perform radical techniques but that is not necessary at all. This can be handled relatively easily."

"Everything is easy, once you understand. Not to say painful."

"Your responses in fact are excellent; your contact is at a very high order. There's no reason to panic at all; we'll have you back and productive in a short time."

I rear on my elbows. The porcelain is hard, the cold slab makes me tremble but nonetheless a point must be made. "I want to get out of here," I say. "I demand that. You have no right to detain me in this fashion; I have a mission to perform and I assure you that you will suffer greatly for what you have done."

He puts his palms together, makes an opening, stares through them at me. "I told you about grandiosity."

"This is serious business," I say, "the very wheel of circumstance is frozen at this moment; it cannot turn until I have worked this through. Detention would be at your peril; you know not what you do. Take off these bindings."

"No," he says, "under the circumstances we have the right to retain you as we must. You would be dangerous to yourself, let alone others if you were released. Anything could happen. I am being very frank with you, nothing is being held back, and you are in no condition to rejoin the community. Surely you would admit to that if you thought about it for a while."

"I'm thinking about it. Let me go."

"I urge you to be calm. That would be for the best. Nothing can hurt you but yourself."

"I am very calm," I say. "I know exactly what is going on here." I note that the restraints are metal, not the leather which they simulate and that as I lift myself against them they dig into my torso as I flail. I stretch on the porcelain, trying to vault beyond them but Lazarus's contrivances are not mine; scissors of pain cut merrily through my trunk and I subside, gasping. "All right," I say, "all right."

"It is better not to resist."

"You will find that will happen to you," I say, "you will see what this means, you will learn the cost of such measures and the judgement which will sit upon you throughout eternity. All of the shapes and creatures of the Last Judgement will observe you and they will know."

The Counselor sighs. "Some of you are not reasonable at the beginning," he says.

"I'm quite reasonable."

"Some of you fight the truth with all your strength. I had hoped that this would not be the case with you but apparently it is. You will fight the truth for a while but all you are doing is delaying your own recovery."

"They said that to Joseph," I say, "but I am not him. Everything is changed. It is a different age."

"Who is Joseph?" the Counselor says. He seems genuinely puzzled. For all of their devices they do not know what is happening here. It is a madness, but part of the inconstancy with which I must live and through which I will walk the path of redemption.

"A betrayed man," I say. "But only in the best of causes," I hurriedly add.

"Am I my brother's keeper?" I say, rudely. "I have my own problems in this wretched land; I can't be responsible for everything; I have a miserable portion of land to till and very little assistance. How do I know where Abel went?"

Sadly Adam says, "I've never seen the land of Nod. I wouldn't even know the way." He takes my mother's hand. "We're going to miss you," he says.

"Miss me? What are you talking about?"

My mother begins to cry. "It's not fair!" she says, "it's not fair, not fair!" and begins to tear at the thatched walls of the hut, "over and over and over again and for what I ask you? For what? To be someone's parable, to be instructive of fools? There must be an end to this!"

My father puts an arm around her and gently leads her away, talking to her quietly, intensely. It is not my affair. None of this is my affair. Quickly, brutally, I gather my few possessions and prepare for my journey to that blasted and empty land.

Tormented by the anguish on the Magdalene's face, the tears which unbidden leak down her cheeks he says, "It is all right. The past, anyone's past, does not matter: all that matters is what happens in the timeless present, the eternal future." He raises a hand, strokes her cheek, feels a strange absent tenderness working within him, almost hammering, beating at the walls of self and this surprises him in its intensity: it is of a different, softer kind than that which he has felt through his earlier travels. That was for the people but this is for a person; there seems to be a difference. From the general to the specific; all pain measured in the cry of one woman. "Come," he says, "you can join me."

She puts her hand against his. "You don't understand," she says, "you're kind, you're wonderful, but this you do not understand. You are too good, perhaps; you would have to be one like me to know. What you offer is not what I want."

"I offer you a practical and perfect peace," I say, "that is what everyone wants."

"Then you don't know anything," she says. "You are a kind man, a saint, a prophet perhaps but of these people, of myself you know nothing at all." She smoothes her garments with a free hand. "You do not know how they regard you."

"And how is that?"

"Do you want the truth?" she says, "then the truth is that to them you are merely a diversion, an element of entertainment in their lives which are otherwise quite empty. They have nowhere to go, nowhere to sleep so they might as well follow you. You amuse them; you sculpt passionate configurations; the only passion they know otherwise is rut so they will listen. But they do not understand your practical and perfect peace and if they thought that this was the true outcome they would leave you and follow someone else."

"I don't think that is true."

"Then you are going to be deeply hurt."

"Of course I'm going to be hurt," I say, astonished. "Don't you know that? That's why I'm here. That's precisely the *point,* to be hurt, Mary." I have never used her given name before. "Mary, practical and perfect peace emerges from the stations of the cross, from the lesson of pain."

"*Jesu,*" she says and my own name is tender on her tongue, "you will not be hurt in the way that you think. Martyrdom will not hurt you; that is, after all, what you seek. It will be something else, something otherwise."

Something otherwise, he thinks. *Something else I think.* In the blasted land with Satan there had been that kind of insight but it had been something else, different; it had slid away. "I don't know," he says, "I can only enact what is destined. It is not for me to say otherwise."

She squeezes my hand, smiles at me. "All right," she says, "if you want it to be that way. You are a wise man; perhaps you do understand; if not you will come to do that. I know nothing beside you after all; I am a harlot."

"Do not refer to yourself that way."

"All right," she says again. "I'm agreeable to that." She is an attractive woman, not without elements of sympathy but staring at her with the word *harlot* in my mind I think that she was of course a prostitute until recently, a prostitute who committed dark acts of which I have no knowledge and that it could be said to be an insolence that she of all people is granting her Saviour such rebuke. Not that I take it personally, to be sure. I try to take nothing personally.

"Come," I say then. "We should return." I could have noted that we have been having this dialogue of repudiation and discovery by a river bank, the muddy waters of the river arching over the concealed stones, the little subterranean animals of the river whisking their way somewhere toward the north, the stunted trees of this time holding clumps of birds which eye us mournfully but with a certain sense of discretion. "It is best if we get back to town now," I say, "don't you think so?"

"No, I don't think so. It's peaceful here and that is what you wanted to give me, right? I could stay out here with you for a long while and it would hurt no one."

"It might hurt."

"Why?"

"Because if we remain out here for a long time talking like this some might misapprehend."

"I don't care. I told you, they're a bunch of peasants. If they don't have one thing to think about, then they will have another. If they do not follow you, then they will follow someone else; if they do not mock me they will find one among themselves to mock. Their opinion is of no concern to me."

"But it must be to me. They are my flock and I their shepherd and I must feed my flock."

"Oh my," Mary says, "my oh my you are a strange man. A wonderful man certainly, a prophet perhaps, but you are the strangest man I have ever known in my life. And I have known more of them than I would truly have wanted."

"That is because I am not a man," I say, "I have told you that. I am in fact—"

"You take all of this so *seriously*," she says, "can't you permit yourself to go through any part of the day without *thinking;* can't you allow things merely to occur without looking for the meaning in them? Perhaps there is no meaning. Perhaps most of it is simply to happen in its own time and way."

"That is what I cannot permit to happen."

"So serious," she says again and reaches toward me, a seductive impact in the brush of her hand, seductive clatter in her breath, and oh my Father indeed it is a strange feeling to see what passes between us then. The sensations are remarkable and of the most dangerous sort. I can hardly bear to consider implication. With halt and stuttering breath I hurl myself upright, thrust Mary away and run stumbling toward Galilee. Behind me it cannot be the sound of her laughter which pursues, oh it cannot be that, tell me that it is not that for I cannot, I cannot, I cannot—

Seem to move this stone from the wall of the tomb to uncover the light. I am alive and beating in this terrible darkness, restored to condition and I know somehow that this as has been promised is a wondrous and complete act and that all that I need do is to stutter into the light *but I cannot remove the stone;* I scramble at it with fingertips, trying to get it to release, trying to open the tomb but it lies heavy against the opening; it must be several hundredweight this stone and feeble and unavailing my efforts to open it. "Help!" I shriek within the barrier, "help, I'm alive in here, someone must take me out!" but my throat, stiff and dry from days of death cannot grant purchase to the air, cannot give voice and the syllables murmur away, "Someone must help me!" I say but the voice is that of a child and I understand that it cannot possibly be heard. Have I been restored, has all prophecy been made flesh simply to take me to this outcome? Oh it would be a mockery, it would mock everything but this may very well be the case. My life is replete with irony, my life is a paradigm of all lives at all times everywhere and creation would lead inevitably to decline, obliteration to renewal, "Oh my, oh my," I say quietly, "I seem to be trapped here," and having said that, having been granted in that utterance a perfect and practical peace however transitory—because I have faced the truth—I slide quietly to the position of penitence and wait for the arc of the night to gather and enclose, to compress and spirit me away. Because I, no more than they, I no less than they, know not what I do nor can grant light to my condition.

"Fools," I say. My fingers hurtle through the sacred, impenetrable text, looking for the proper citation. I know I will find it in just a moment. In the moment, in the twinkling of an eye. At the last trumpet. "Can't you understand that you are living at the end of time? The chronologies of the Book of Daniel clearly indicate that the seven beasts emerge from the seven gates in the year 2222." And we shall all be raised. Be raised incorruptible. "The numbers are aligned; it is this generation which will know the gathering of the light nor any to follow."

They stare at me with interest but without conviction. They are stupid; I should have known this from the start. "You had better attend," I say. "You have little time, little enough time to repent and it will go much easier for you, for me and the rest of us if you do so at the outset."

A congregant raises his hand tentatively, holds it patiently until I am forced to recognize him. He stands, a shrunken old man wrapped in tallis and phylacteries and steps toward me. "Rabbi," he says, "you are suffering from a terrible misapprehension which I must call to your attention."

"So are you all," I say calmly. "The human condition is misapprehension; we impute meanings that are unique to the generalized. Nonetheless we struggle on."

"No, Rabbi, it is not that at all. I must tell you that this is not Bruck Linn and the Book of Daniel has nothing to do with what is happening."

"Fool," I say. I struggle against a certain impression of twine; I seem to be bound, lashed prone by coils of rope. "You may conceive of a pogrom but that does not make the pogrom happen. Only the assassins may bring it about but none of their murders will delay the oncoming of the apocalypse." I am exhausted by this statement; I stumble back from the podium in exhaustion, the sensation of rope fading. It is hard to tell exactly what is going on.

"Rabbi," the elderly man says, gesturing with a forefinger, "there is no oncoming apocalypse. And furthermore you are not a rabbi. You are—"

I shout in rage, slam against the podium and feel the twine once again. They curl back in their chairs showing terror; the elderly man scuttles to the back of the room. "Wrong!" I shriek, "wrong, wrong!" I grip the Pentauch firmly and hurl it to the midst of the congregation. The pages open like a bird's wing in flight but the air takes it and it flutters pointlessly against an opposing wall, falls with all the impact of dust. "I have my duties," I say, "I have my obligations. You had better let me go out and deliver the summons to the world; you had better attend to me. Ignoring me will not keep back the truth, jeering at me will only hasten the time of that great snake. It cannot be masked and I assure you that it will all go much easier for you if you cooperate."

They stare at me with bright, beady eyes. Some of them are impressed but others are not and it is possible for me as always to tell the difference. I can tell my enemies; in any gathering it is possible for me to pick out those who will defend me and those who would betray. It is an ability which comes with the mastery of Talmudic lore and will save me from annihilation in the future.

"You are sick, Rabbi," the elderly man says quietly from the back. He pats the fringe on his tallis, twirls the strands. "You are a very sick man. It is good that you are receiving the treatment that you so desperately need. The treatment is for your own good, Rabbi and at this very moment they are working to help you but you must trust them."

"The great snake," I point out, "the great snake which lies coiled in the guard of gates—"

"Rest, Rabbi. Close your eyes, submit to the treatments. They will soothe you, cleanse your soul; everything will pass much easier for you."

"That great snake is slowly rising," I say, he is shaking off the sleep of the ten thousand, evading the guardians of the gate, planning his swift and terrible course. It may only be a *cheder* in Bruck Linn but from simple and humble surroundings was it foresaid that the world would travel forth.

At this moment the dust of the apocalypse awaits all of you unless you heed—"

"A holy book."

"What?" I say, stunned, stopped in mid-discourse. "What are you talking about?"

The old man stoops, circles on the floor like a hound, straightens with the Pentauch in his hand. "You have thrown a holy book," he says. "How can you adjudge yourself to be a keeper of the word if you throw a book at the congregation?"

"No. No books are holy," I say. I summon all my powers of concentration to the response, a gift for Talmudic disputation has never been more necessary than at this moment. *No books are holy.* At the end of time, awaiting the pitiless and terrible judgement, even the sacred texts must fall away. All that will be left is judgement, the absence of grace, the deprivation of mercy, the high winds rising, the merciless stones, the darkness—"

"If you could only relax, Rabbi," the elderly congregant says earnestly, "if you would only try to take the long view here, understand that matters are not nearly as painful as you make them appear, calm and submit to the restraints you would find that things would be so much easier." He tilts his yarmulka, gives a gentle and implicatory wink. "We're all in this together, after all," he says, "not you against the congregation but rather all of us congregants. The times call not for passion but for community."

"Community?" I say, "what do you know of community? For a thousand years you have invoked the word only as the alternative to persecution. We have gone beyond that, the times are desperate, we must walk to and fro on the earth and up and down upon it!" I cough mightily, hawk phlegm in my excitement. "From all of these wanderings I will come to a fuller knowledge, crouching then at the end of time with the old, cold, bold antagonist to cast lots over the vestments of the saved and unjudged alike, bargaining for their garments out of which a different and better world will be stitched, awaiting the renewed colors of renewed circumstance—"

"If you will only be quiet, Rabbi. If you will only be calm, it will be so much easier—"

"The snake is quiet too," I say, "the snake is deprived of speech and posture, music and stature by that ancient curse and it is his silence which we must battle through our speech. His silence crests toward the day of judgement, it is that to which he would have us submit, that to which all the forces of the darkness would carry us but let me tell you, let me tell you that this silence which you demand is not that of renewal but that of the void itself. We must speak, we must make sound against the void, we must create a language of the night which will fill all the spaces with the sound of our voices and—"

And. And what? I listen to myself carry on, listen to all the bumbling and reiterative syllables with which I try to make the case to congregants who will never understand, observe myself flail against a body of congregants who will not be moved. Je ne sais pas. I simply do not know. It is wearying even at this remove to repeat all of those admonitions which continue to rave through the spaces of the room, words like insects fluttering about, landing to no purpose, changing nothing. They look at me stupidly. They know not what they do. They have absolutely no comprehension of the situation and that will never change.

If there is one thing to be said about a Talmudic authority in full speech it is that once launched toward a point he can hardly pause. Can hardly pause. Pauses would form interstices where the golem itself would perch. And of the golem itself, of course, the sacred texts are filled; utter testimony is available on the difficult and painful subject and nothing, therefore, need be said at all. No testimony is necessary. The golem is of a different tradition and can well speak for itself. *Je renounce.*

Of the earlier affectionals nothing can be said. Some ended emotionlessly and some with affect but all can be said to have ended badly. In and out of these things one carries only the purchase of self; one must replicate oneself in all the corridors and none of the affectionals were able to shift the balance as I thought Edna would, as I thought at the beginning might be possible. In those first weeks of our connection I found in her great expressivity some demonstration of my own; felt that she would help me wedge free of myself but later as we began to fall against rather than into one another I came to understand that this could not be so and that she was merely another of a series of failed, sometimes disastrous attempts, to change that part of me which could not be reached other than by the hypnotics. Which was why I took myself to the technicians without her previous knowledge and made the arrangements, which was why I returned to tell her that this was what had to be done without conferring with her first.

Her aspect was pained. "You should not have done this, Harold," she said, "at least you should have spoken to me?" I had expected this. "Why didn't you let me know?"

"It had nothing to do with you."

"The lovelies bleeding," she said, "but who were the lovelies? And who is bleeding?"

"We're all bleeding," I said, "the century is bleeding." Looking at her I felt whispers of the way it had been at the outset, staring at those dark, pained eyes that seemed to open up to an insight deeper than I had ever known. I remembered how it had been when I felt that she was the last of affectionals and would restore me. How little I had known to think that what had never been done could be restored; that the unmade could be reclaimed. "I'm bleeding," I said.

"It's dangerous and futile. Don't you know that? Many who have gone through it have become mad."

"I won't go crazy. That can't happen to me."

"You don't know that until you live it, Harold. It's too dangerous. You know the stories. For my sake, don't do it," she said. She took my hand. "It will be different between us. It could be better."

"I don't believe that any more," I said, "nothing can be any better unless you start at the beginning."

"I know stories," she said intensely, "I've known people who have gone through it. They're never the same again. Some of them have gone away forever."

"Are you afraid I'll go away forever? Do you want me to leave you, Edna?"

"Oh Harold," she said, "you're such a fool, you really understand nothing, nothing at all and yet you take yourself so seriously that it's impossible for you to learn." Her expression became solemn, turned inward. "Do as you must," she said, "I can't stop you. It's your decision."

"Will you stay with me?"

"Where? In the treatment room?"

"You know what I mean, Edna."

"I'll stay with you, Harold," she said, "you see, I have absolutely nowhere else to go so I'll stay for a while. It doesn't make any difference, you see. It doesn't make any difference where I am; the process must begin inside. That's something that you'll find out."

"And that is what I'm doing," I said, "I'm working from the inside. They will change me from the inside."

"You understand nothing," she said, "nothing whatsoever."

And the lovelies reaching, blooming, bleeding in the night. And all the lovelies bleeding.

"Will you yield?" Satan says. He forces me to an untenable position upon the sands, puts pressure on a dangerous lock, drags my arm unbearably behind, stopping at the median point of pain. His great face looms near mine like a lover's, in its crevices I see eternity. He seems about to implant the most sustained and ominous of kisses. "Yield and it will go much easier with you. You can bring all of this to an end with a word."

Old tempter; old accomplice. "No," I say, "never. I will not yield. It is not only my burden which I carry but that of eternity." The French has departed, likewise the depersonalization and at last I feel as one with the persona which is a very good sign. Surely it is at least a sign that I have moved closer to the accomplishment of my great mission.

"You may torture me," I say as the slivers of pain from the half-broken arm gather into me like shrapnel, "you may torture, you may bring all of your strength to bear, it is possible that you will bend and break me but you will never hear renunciation. I give nothing to you."

I scramble in the sands, twist, manage to forage a little bit of space as the clutch on my arm dwindles. In just a moment I will try a surprise attack; I am not out of possibilities yet. "And if I did give up," I say to distract him, "what difference would it make? My weight is as the weight of all the centuries, there would only be another in time to take my place. And then another. You may deal with us piecemeal but you cannot change the condition; always the light and darkness will be joined."

"Sophistry," he says, "sophistry," and increases pressure on my wrist to bring up the arm; with a sly wrench I drag him toward me instead, defy his sense of balance. He grunts, a knee brushes my back and then the hold is released and he is tumbled beside, lies against me on the sands. My arm is free. He groans, the exhalation of breath full as dead flowers in my face and it is possible for me now to hurl myself all the way over him, pressing him onto the sands. "You're not so smart, you see?" I whisper, "you're not what you think you are at all; things can be done."

Gasping, he rears to his knees, reaches, attempts to toss me behind but cunningly I fall on top of him. My knee strikes his horned and shaven head, administering a stunning blow. *"Ah!"* he says, *"ah!"*, fluid bubbling deep in his throat and from the cut I have opened on his scalp I see springing the delicate, discolored blood of Satan. It bursts upon him and falls in looping threads to the sand, blood not unlike mine but containing solid material. His eyes flutter to attention and then astonishment as I close upon him. My strength is legion; I have made my mark upon him just as he has upon me. "Do you see?" I say, "do you see now what you have done? You cannot win against the force of light, the prince of peace, the counsellor, the lion of Judea. The government shall be upon my shoulder." He murmurs something.

I prepare to deliver the blow of vanquishment. I realize that he is helpless and this perception is his as well; I can see him take the insight, absorb it, gasp with the knowledge as it bites through the plates of his being. The blood has stopped to a small ooze; his respiration is enormous. "It must be done," I say, "there can be no alternative."

"Stop," he says weakly. He raises a taloned

hand. "Stop now, you must."

To my surprise I do so. I would not have thought that I could be so easily dissuaded. On the other hand there is no hurry now; he is completely within my power. All of them are completely within my power. "That's better," he says, "at least you can hear reason when it is given to you. Now you're to stop this nonsense at once, do you understand that?"

"Stop it?" I say. "Stop what nonsense? What are you talking about? This is apocalypse here."

"Apocalypse," Satan says. He grunts. "Put out a hand and help me stand."

"Absolutely not. I know your trickery but am invulnerable to it."

"You're not listening, you fool. You don't know what this means; this dispute was supposed to be purely dialectical. No one was to suffer physical injury. Study the prophets, the sacred texts and you'll understand."

Ah, the cunning. The cunning of Satan! Defeated on his own terms he would of course shift the ground but I have been prepared for this as well. I have been fully prepared for all the flounderings of the ancient and clever enemy: there is nothing that he can do now to dissuade and so I laugh at him, secure in my own power. "Dialectical?" I say.

"Of course—"

"Of course not. I knew the terms. It was a struggle unto death which had been foresaid and you knew that as well as I for if I had not turned advantage you would have killed me."

"No," he says. He shakes his head, a drop of blood flies, I observe the dull and drying scar already bleached by the desert sun. "No, absolutely not; you never saw this right. This was not a matter of murder, can't you see? We aren't antagonists at all! We're two aspects of the self, our search was for fusion in these spaces and that is now what we are prepared to do."

"Fusion?" I say, "you're talking of the Trinity, of the conception, not of this."

"That's all display," he says, "distraction." His head sinks, he is clearly exhausted. These struggles have drained him as has the fear, at last of death. "You fool," he says quietly, "there is no way that either of us can vanquish the other. For either to kill either is to destroy the self."

"The self?"

"We are bound, linked. We are the two parts set against one another. That is what they have done to us for their amusement and our anguish."

Sophistry! Dialectic, materialism! I am so sick of it all; I intimate a life, a dark passage through to the end of it all lit only by the flickering and evil little candles of half-knowledge and witticism, casting ugly pictures, casting the stones themselves and the image engages me at a certain level: it would be a life devoid of purpose but also of pain. One could nest within the coils of the old deceiver, the great Comforter and forget what one was put on the earth to do; one could find in that circumstance conversion of hatred to resignation, passion to resolution.

But no, no. No to all of that: I cannot bear the

thought of a life which will contain little more than small alterations of language or perception to make it bearable, reconsideration of a constant rather than to change the irretrievable constant itself. *This* is to what I have been condemned and it can be no other way. Satan may live by rhetoric but I will die by blood.

And here at least, on this desert, rhetoric will not prevail, speech will not be the only end. Perhaps for the only time in my life, in all lives, I will have the opportunity to undertake the single purposeful act. A commission of circumstance rather than intellection. Death rather than denial.

And so, feeling that moment press upon me, feeling its weight and fearing that it will crush unless I move quickly I wheel upon Satan fiercely. "I've had enough of this shit," I say, "I really have; I've got to deal with it. I cannot go on like this forever, there simply has to be a time for confrontation."

To myself I seem a bit confused but my action is not nor is it confusing. I plunge a foot into his face. It yields in a spatter of bone, an enormous firmament of blood and he screams, then falls away. I look upon his truest form. It is not exactly what I would have expected but then deception is part of his case and it could have been no other way.

"Well," Satan says through flopping jaw. "Well, well, well. Look at you. Look at both of us. I'll be damned."

"Oh yes," I say, "yes you will, but you don't have to take all of us with you. It is possible for some of us to be saved; there are no universals."

His eye, surprisingly mild, radiates, of all things,

compassion. "You still don't understand," he says. He clambers to his knees like a great, stricken bird. "After having gone this far you don't understand anything at all."

"I do enough," I say, "by far."

"I'm not here by choice. I'm here because you *want* me. I was called upon; I'm performing a function. Do you think that this is easy? Being thrown out of Heaven and walking up and down the spaces of the earth and to and fro upon it, the plagues and the cattle and the boils and the awful depressions, the recrimination, the self-loathing? That's the part of you that you don't want to face and I've had to take all of it upon myself, my burden, it was you who brought me to being as the furnace in which you would ignite and shrivel all of you that you could not bear and I've just been so busy, so used up in the process as you might expect but then again—"

He rolls to one side, brings his legs up, flings a claw against them. Blood has soaked his chest, mingled with the scales to produce an aspect and odor of putrefaction. "Then again," he says, "this could be rationalization. I'm aware of that too; I'm good at sophistry, you know, that was always my specialty, the force of the will you gave me but this isn't easy you know. There's a lot of pain in this, the texts give me no advantage but I don't find it any easier than the martyrs, a lot worse in fact because the martyrs at least have a good reputation. I'm in pain, I'm suffering: I have feelings as well. I am the sum of everything loathsome and denied within you; how could I not have feelings?"

I stand, considering him. What he is saying is very complex and doubtless I should attend to it more closely. (In fact, I sense that it would save me the most atrocious difficulty later on if only I would) but there is a low and teasing sense of accomplishment in having dealt with this assignment so effectively and I do not want to deny myself its conclusion so easily. Nothing is done until it is committed; I do not want to run even the slightest risk that persuasion may shift desire. It may be one of the least equivocal moments for me in a life riven, as we all know, by conflicts. Ambivalence is for Paul, for Simon Peter, for Timothy; it is not for me. I am a simple, kindly, brutal man; a man of peasant stock and easy design.

"I'm dying," Satan says, "Won't you at least reach out a hand to comfort me at the end? We share the bond of our belief if nothing else. Who would take us seriously?"

The appeal is grotesque and yet I am moved. He is, after all, and as he says, a creature of circumstance no less than any of the rest of us. I kneel beside him quickly, trying not to betray revulsion at the putrefaction, the rotting flesh that falls in clumps from his face exposing the great horns and the truest form. "Hold me," he says, "you owe me at least that, you know you do. You called me into being, you asked me to serve your purposes, you have to take responsibility for my vanquishment. Or are you seeking to deny complicity?"

"*Deny* complicity? The whole purpose of this was to accept it," I say.

"Well, at least that shows some progress," the

expiring Satan says. "I can respect that and if I were immune to pain as the Testaments falsely decree I would even show a little pleasure. Unfortunately I am *not* immune to pain and I am at this moment in the most excruciating anguish. Give me your hand."

"My hand?"

"Now," Satan says, "it is my last request and you know that it is proper."

I do so. I extend my hand. His claw, my fingers interlock. The binding is intense; it is as if we were meant from the beginning to meld into one another. *I should have known it would be this way.* Captured by one another, our limbs are indistinguishable; it is hard to tell where the one begins, the other ends. Blood bubbles from his skull; a wicker of absolution comes from his lips.

"You see?" Satan says gratefully, "do you see now? You *know* at least that you're implicated, that you are part of this now. There may be some hope in that for all of us and now if you will permit me, if you will be so kind, Nazarene, I believe that I am going to die. You won't mind that, will you? I wish that I could say that I will do it in the very best of taste but I am afraid that I cannot; I am, to be sure, in awful pain."

He retches. Bubbles come from his mouth; heaving little rivulets of grey and greenish blood. They pour from his nasal passages, his eyes and ears as well. The greenish, ruined blood springs to the desert floor and I stare fascinated. "It isn't very pretty, is it?" he whispers. I lean closer. "As the Prince of Darkness himself, I will tell you that there is nothing aseptic or admirable about death. Death hurts, death is disgusting; death is the act of passage into the unspeakable and of itself must therefore be," Satan says wisely and for the first time then I feel sympathy for him; whatever he is or has been he has paid for that condition justly. I raise my hand in benediction.

He winks, sighs, nods and dies. His last sounds are quick, muffled little sighs not unlike the sounds of love. It is an enormous and dignified accomplishment, his death, the Scriptures have hardly taken proper note of it and I am bound by the spectacle for more than a few moments. Kneeling beside him I whisper the prayer of my Father and it is a spellbinding and shattering occasion for only at the moment of release can I perceive that his spirit too is entitled to divine unction. I take his claw, collapsed now in passage and squeeze it, then bring it to my lips. In that dark kiss I feel our fate congealed forever.

But then I must drop his claw; then I must abandon touch. All things must go away as has been pointed out, not only flesh but circumstance is grass. Letting his claw slide I have a vision and in that brief vision I see what might have saved me all of this motion. There was another way that it could have been handled. There was, all the time, another option which I did not seek.

Knowing that, perceiving it sadly, there is a consequent wrench in my own corpus which echoes an indicating, smaller death and as I realize then that he has told me the truth—and did I not know that he would always tell me the truth?—and that the elimination of Satan has only resulted in a reduction of the self I stand in the desert, stunned.

Stunned, gentlemen, oh fathers and confessors all, stunned, knowing now that none of this—and I above all am here to give the testimony—none of this was ever as simple as I thought.

Nor will it ever be.

We are implicated in everything. We *are* everything. Everything that moves and breathes, streaks and sighs is part of us.

And will never end.

"You knew it," Edna says. She leans over me. Apparently they have brought her to the mosque to give me words of advice or then again this may be a table in the Institute. Or Mount Ararat. Who is to tell? "All of the time you knew that it would end this way. You plunged into it. You love it, you son of a bitch, you love every ounce of the pain, you wouldn't know what to do without it but this time you've taken on more than you can handle."

Hands appear and begin to ease her away. Apparently this was not what she was expected to say. "I don't care!" she screams, "he's got to have the truth, even if it kills the stupid son of a bitch he's dead already, he might as well have the truth, shouldn't he? *You* did it, not the Confessors, the overseers, the wires or the hypnotics; *you* put yourself here." She is taken out of sight. I strain to see her but my head is bound and I cannot move; my vision is blurred, my hands are tied and my heart, my heart, o Lord my heart is heavy and dense within me.

* * *

"Ruined cattle, dead sons, empty counting house, pustules and boils," my wife says, "You caused all of this." Apparently the women in my life seem to have reached a certain unanimity of opinion. "You can hang out in the fields with your Comforters all day and listen to their lies but the simple truth of the matter is that you wanted the plagues and the pain, you needed it for some part of yourself and you're not going to be excused from that. You won't curse God and die? Well, that's your decision but I've had enough of this. I won't stay here and watch the plagues tear me apart; I'm not going to sit and scratch your boils and tell you what a just man you are. Do you understand?" she says, "This is the end." It appears to be the end. She turns from me. I wonder exactly how I will be able to put this to the Comforters so that they will see my side of the question.

"Even the minor prophets have problems," I point out in the mosque. "The fact that I am not famous and that many of my judgements are vague does not mean that they aren't deeply felt or that I will not suffer the fate of Isaiah, second Isaiah, Jeremiah, Zephaniah. Daniel and Solomon did good but they were of a different sort. Ezekiel had a limp and was tormented by self-hatred. Hosea had blood visions and no sleep for years."

They look at me bleakly, those fifteen. This is what my flock has dwindled to and I should be grateful to have them, should have no complaints what with all of the efforts to discredit and those many threats of violence made toward those who would yet remain. They are a courageous bunch, I suppose. But not to deny: they are quite stupid primarily; the brighter ones have long since responded to the pressure but these that persist are all that I have and I am grateful, I suppose to have them even though those that know a correct prophet are already gone. "Attend," I say, "listen to me, the institutions cannot remain in this condition. Their oppression is already the source of its own decay; they panic, they can no longer control the uprising. The inheritors of these institutions are stupid; they do not know why they work or how but just mechanically reiterate the processes for their own fulfillment, massacre to protect themselves, oppress because oppression is all they know of the machinery. But their time is limited, the wind is rising and the sounds of revolution will overtake the land—"

And so on. So forth. Drain me as circumstance might, the rhetorical turns and flourishes will never desert me; they can be done so skillfully that they occupy only the most fleeting part of my attention. Enraptured by passion I have a reduced need for circumstance but in this business one learns to handle circumstance with inattention or not at all. I listen to the sound of my voice, observe the bleak and staring aspect of my congregation but what I am actually doing is considering the door.

It is the door which I am giving a great deal of thought. It was not locked, a stupid, daring gesture but now I wish very much that I had taken the time and trouble to do so even if it had panicked the congregation. That door bulges, it clatters open and through it enter three men in the dress of my sect but I have never seen them before and from some furtive, heightened expression in their eyes I suspect that they have not come here on a merciful business. They must have bought the dress from some of my deserted followers, either bought or stolen it. The last of them in the room closes the door delicately, directs the others to stand against a far wall. In a row they lean, consulting with one another in low tones and it is all that I can do, seeing this, to continue speaking.

But I must continue speaking. I must not show a lapse of rhetoric, let them know that I suspect them in any way because all that I hold is the prospect of my inattention. "Consider the Keepers," I say, "and how they were overthrown; it is decades ago and yet the lessons of that time apply fully to what we know today, they can be reapplied. The Keepers were overthrown and we were promised freedom but how much has really changed? In their time it was done by outright slaughter, now it is in a kinder fashion, one is not put to death by the state so much as absorbed by it, permitted to use the devices for annihilation but it is all the same, the same history of exploitation and I tell you that we must work anew. We must replicate the struggle, the overthrow." What am I saying? What is all of this about? My prose rolls and thunders but it means nothing at all; I seem to be calling for revolution but all that absorbs me is the possibility of flight. I am already considering the way out of here. "Take the state down by challenging it direct," I say but as I murmur about challenge, scream about overthrow it is exit which I am considering. I must get out of here. Obviously this bunch does not wish me well and are making plans for my removal. One picks up certain perceptions in this business. Prophecy can be a business of close as well as far range. One learns to protect oneself if only in order to continue to prophesy.

But my alternatives are, to say the least, limited. The windows are barred, the walls are blank behind me, the only exits are at the edge of the hall and why didn't I bar the door? In the dwindling of my congregation I have lost the guards of course, they were among the first whose lack of faith led them to leave, and it was stupid of me not to create any security for myself. A characteristic stupidity, of course, self-destructiveness must also be part of this business.

"Be strong," I say to my dozing congregants, "be brave, master your fears, overcome the Keepers, do not allow them to intimidate you for their power can be broken by simple defiance," but I do not feel very strong or brave at all. "Fight them, confer with one another, form groups, do not allow them to divide you," I am saying but I feel utterly perplexed and filled with fear which is very close to self-loathing. I never conferred with anyone; I wanted to keep all of the proceeds for myself . . . there was so little to divide that I felt entitled to it all. "It will not be easy," I say, "but nothing worthwhile of course was ever accomplished easily." This is a truism. My sermon has collapsed to platitude and cliche and yet there seems to be absolutely nothing to be done about it.

Their conference concludes and the three men scatter quickly. One goes toward a seat in the center of the room, the other two nod at one another and part, slide against the walls. They fumble inside their clothing, either in search of an itch or to check the availability of firearms. I am pretty sure that it is the firearms. I always knew they would come with guns.

They are assassins, then, no doubt about it and they have been on my trail for so very long that it would stand to reason that at last they would be in this room but I am in a unique and difficult position. If I demonstrate fear, if I react to their presence they will doubtless slay me in the mosque, causing the most unusual consternation to the few followers assembled but on the other hand if I proceed through the speech and toward an orderly dismissal all that will happen is that I will make their method of murder more convenient and allow for an absence of witnesses. Then too I could continue to prophesy, prophesy and speak but it is exhausting and at a certain point my rhetoric not to say my constitution will give out. There are limits to the power to invent.

In short, anything I do is calculated to work against me and yet I am a man who has always believed in dignity, the dignity of position that is to say, taking a stand, following it through whatever the implications. Once I have found a position, however untenable, I find it necessary to carry it through; nothing less seems worthy of me, and so I continue, I continue, my rhetoric is perhaps a shade florid now, my sentences not as routinely parsed as I would wish but it is no go, no go, no go at all: they have a different method I see as the seated one arises and moves briskly toward me. It is only then that the chain of rhetoric breaks and I find myself coming outside of the focus of my will.

"Now listen," I say, "this is not right, not right at all," backing under his grasp, "you could at least have let me finished you know; if I was willing to take it to this point then you could have gone along with me."

The congregants murmur. One of them accuses me of disloyalty. This seems quite ridiculous, I would like to point out; if anyone has been disloyal it is they, why are they not defending me? Surely they should respond to an attack upon their leader. But I have never *been* their leader, something that I should have realized a long time ago. I have been a diversion.

"Harold," the man grasping my arm says, "Harold you had better come with me."

I try to shrug him off. His grip, however, is insistent. Is it possible that I am dreaming this? It is very doubtful; dreams would not have this constancy or threat. "Take your hands off me," I say, "this is not reasonable."

"That is why we are here."

"Get away from me," I say, "at least let me finish. See how they're looking at me? They need prophesy, information: I'm doing the best that I can here to give it to them. You at least could let me finish."

"You're finished, Harold. You're finished all right."

"Leave me alone!" I say. My voice is penitent, submissive, I am disgusted with myself, filled with revulsion. "Leave me alone, now, get out of here!"

"We'd best not do that," he says gently, "that isn't really what you want at all." He gestures toward the two in the rear who begin to walk toward me solemnly. "We're going to take care of you. Everything will be better."

"Nothing will be better."

"What we're going to do," he says soothingly, "what we must do here is to jolt you out of these little fugues, these tiny essays in martyrdom and take you back to the world in which you will occupy your own and rightful role. It would be best if you cooperated, Harold; the more you cooperate, the quicker you will see the evidence of reality and the more quickly you will be back to yourself."

This remark seems to penetrate; it has an emotional force at any rate. "I don't want to be back to myself," I say. "I want to be right here."

"You can't be right here, Harold," the man says almost cheerfully. "Here is no place to be and surely you have deduced that by now. Come," he says, giving me a hearty little pat on the flank, a merry tug, "let's just bounce out of here now, get you started, get things in motion," and the other two come fore and aft and quite forcefully propel me from the rostrum.

"Are you going to let me be carried away like this?" I say to my congregants, "are you just going to let them do that? Can't you see what is happening here?"

They stare at me, shuffle their feet. They are not a courageous bunch but then how could they be:

they have elected to listen to the ravings of a tenth-rate fanatic. "They don't want you to know the truth!" I shout at them nonetheless, "They don't want you to accept the truth of your lives; that's why they're carrying me out of here, because I was leading you to it."

This does not appear to make any impression. "You fools," I say, "I'm just trying to help you!" I gesticulate wildly. My motions are frenzied; they lack any constancy of rhythm. "They're dragging me out of here on your behalf! Aren't you going to defend me?" I scream, "This isn't fair; I am entitled to support from my congregants, you can't allow me to take responsibility for your lives."

"Now, now, Harold," one of them says as I am dragged through the doors, "calm down, all of this has its place but after a while it's just best to cooperate, just go along, just meet the needs and desires of the state, we're only trying to help you, you know that it's for the best," and now they have dragged me through the doors, not a one, not a single one of my congregants making the slightest attempt to fracture their progress. "All for the best, all for the best," they say and begin to use their strength. It is insistent; I understand that all of the time until now they had been mollifying. I never had a chance at all.

I curse my congregants. "You sons of bitches," I say, "don't any of you care, don't you know what's going on here, don't you know what this is?" and so on and so forth and on and on and on, the sounds of my rhetoric filling my ears, if hardly all of the world and outside I am plunged strongly, repeatedly into the brackish waters of Galilee which to no one's surprise at all (or at least not to mine for I know almost everything now) hardly lend absolution.

There is no absolution.

None at all.

"You'll see," Satan points out, flicking an ash off his cigar and leaning back comfortably, "you'll see just how upright, faithful and devoted a servant he is if the cattle start to drop and the counting house empties."

"On the contrary," I say, "his faith has no bounds; it cannot be shaken."

"Would you prefer a contest? Let me deal with the counting house and the cattle and then see what he says."

I shrug, take the bottle from his hand and take a meditative swallow. "What would the stakes be?"

"Do you want stakes? Would you not want to try this merely for intellection?"

The liquor is good; it burns away for the moment the dust of the eternities and I feel a certain skittishness which in the old days I indulged quite often, more often than now I must admit when I find solemnity more in keeping with the tenor of the times, my own observations of inequity and despair, the powerful and unhappy statements of Gomorrah. "All right," I say, "not merely intellection. There must be some consequence involved."

"Good," Satan says. Through the screen of liquor I can see that he is not really a bad fellow; he retains many of those qualities which compelled me to select him for his role in the first place. He is not a bad angel at all at the heart although of course the exigencies of performance have brought out the worst in him. "Would you consider perhaps readmission?"

I squint at him, hoist the bottle. "You mean, letting you back into the fold?"

"That's why I asked."

I tilt the bottle, drink, put it down with a crash against a huge, metallic cloud. "I'm afraid not," I say, "I'm really sorry but that's impossible. You're doing the job so well. Who would possibly replace you? We could never find your match and it would take millennia to train even an inadequate replacement. No, I'm afraid that you'll have to stay."

"Too bad," Satan says, "see? I told you that you set this thing up primarily for your entertainment."

I regard the bottle happily. "Maybe I am and maybe I'm not," I say, "but you'll never know. I'm not admitting anything. I tell you what I'll do though; I'll make the stake my own continuing involvement. If Job loses faith, if he abandons me, then I'll never bother any of them again. I'll disinvolve myself, turn the whole thing over to you. How does that sound?"

"Not too bad," Satan says, "kind of interesting. What if you win, though?"

"If I win, then I'll get even further involved, give you more with which to struggle, keep you even busier."

"How?"

"Oh, I don't know," I say, "I'll think about it." I brood for a while, perhaps six months of Job's life, it is hard to tell but his shoulders when next I observe him are slightly more stooped from carrying coins to their hiding place in the fields. "I'll send my only begotten Son, how about that?"

"I don't understand."

"I'll make myself flesh and dwell among them, have all kinds of experiences. The liturgy which this will create will keep them going for centuries and will make it harder for you. After all, if I give *concrete* evidence of my existence—"

"I understand," Satan says. He takes the bottle back from me, drinks hurriedly, shudders. "Well, it's a difficult situation, a hard circumstance, that's to be sure. On the other hand, I don't think you have a chance to win. So I accept the wager."

"Excellent."

"Can I start the plagues now?" Satan says eagerly. "I've been waiting so long—"

I make a grandiose gesture, lean back, perch on an elbow, observe all circumstance drifting beneath. "Help yourself," I say, "anytime you're ready."

"What a fool," Satan says, considering Job as he attends his cattle, oversees his servants, makes love to his wife, counsels his sons, does commerce with the merchants of his town. "How unaware they are of what's really going on here."

"Would they be any better off if they were aware?"

Satan considers this, rocking his tail back and forth as he tends to do during thoughtful moments. "No," he said, "I think at last we've found something on which we can agree. No, I don't think that we can say they'd be any better off at all."

"Prosit," I say, lifting the bottle of liquor.

"They'd probably be worse," Satan says meditatively.

"Will you listen to reason, Harold?" Edna says as if from a great distance. Her outline is blurry but her voice unmistakable. "Will you stop this, will you come out of it before you do real damage?"

"Come here and hump me, love," I say, "let me see those lovelies bleeding."

She withdraws. In the mist, silence; in the void eternity. I giggle and plunge deeper yet.

"You'd better destroy them," I say in a conversational tone, settling myself more comfortably underneath the gourd. "They're a pretty rotten bunch as you can see."

"I know that. That's why you're here."

"Ain't a one of them that has thought of anything but their own pleasure since I've been here. To say nothing of the sexual perversity. I've never seen so much onanism and improper entrance; it's absolutely disgusting."

"To be sure," he says reasonably, "I knew all this before you did." He is always reasonable which is, to be sure, a good thing if one is engaging in these highly internalized, intense dialogues. At least this contains matters; enables me to appear sane to the populace. What would I do if he were to suddenly lose patience and scream? I could hardly deal with that; my aspect would be lunatic and I am extremely sensitive to heat and light, noise and pain.

"It's fairly drastic," he says, "and besides that, without life there is no possibility of repentance. Only if they observe can they come to know their condition."

"Oh come on," I say, "don't start all of that again. You've sent me all of these miles through heat and water, into and out of the belly of a whale to warn them of doom and now you reconsider? It would put both of us in a pretty ridiculous position, don't you think? They'd never take me seriously again, after all of those warnings and threats. They'd consider that they have license to continue doing exactly what they are for the rest of their lives."

"That part is *my* decision, Jonah," he says, "and falls into my hands alone."

Well, there is no point in arguing with him when he gets into one of these moods. I know all the signs, one cannot argue at all when he becomes stubborn and arbitrary about his role. I know better than to try; the testaments are already rife with tales of those who crossed his will. "We'll see about this in the morning," I say, much as if it were *I* controlling the situation rather than he which is not quite true of course but one must put the best face on matters. I slip, instead, into a thick doze populated with the images of sea and flying fish but as I burrow deeper the sleep opens to the vision of a century of machines and devices which have been constructed so that others may have exactly the experience which I am having now and the vision is quite frightening as could well be imagined. Who would want to have these experiences, who could possibly want to have to deal with a curmudgeon like this who is as likely as not to toss you into the belly of a whale out of pique? I struggle to emerge from this sleep, struggle to emerge into a simpler world in which Nineveh embraces all evil and Tyre is a siege against faith, where great whales can vomit prophets whole and sailors have no more terrible punishment to their hand than casting overboard. Slowly, slowly I turn in the furnace of this state of being, trying to come free from it, looking at freedom from the sleep as a kind of growth but it is intensely difficult, there are months of accumulated exhaustion here and one does not come from even this bitter surcease easily. From here to there I have been driven by this obsessed circumstance who takes my designs very little into account, cares for my bowels and comfort not at all and at the depths of my being when all seemed undone was forced to deliver to Nineveh in the public square a speech of declamation and fury, call down absolute judgement upon them which could not have been well received under any circumstances and still the disputations continue. Fortunately they were too drunk in the town square to take me seriously, otherwise it would have gotten much worse, as it was I could barely make it back to the desert. Thoughts like these carry me, burning, to the crest of sleep and finally I emerge, I come to consciousness or what passes for it and there is terrible pain through the base of being. My head is in anguish, my head feels as if it were carved open, split to the sun and staring upward I see that the gourd which he had so kindly spread for me when I composed myself for slumber has shrivelled overnight. The sun is blood, lapping hugely in the sky, roaring; the heat drenches me like water and I squeal in protest, barely able to bring sound through the enlarged tissues of the throat. Truly I have been placed in an unspeakable, humiliating condition; after months of whales, sailors and stones this is the most humiliating of all casts.

"Art thou very angry?" I hear him say. He is always there; that voice dwells within me with the horrid intimacy of bowels or phlegm, to resume a dialogue with him is merely to replicate the self. Indeed I feel that he might be the self; he seems to have this effect upon the prophets or at least those whose fates that I have studied. It is not so much visitation as presence, an absent twitch of the familiar at all times. "Tell me," he says to my silence and his voice is demanding, "I wish to know, Jonah. Speak to me. Art thou very angry?"

"Of course I am very angry," I say.

"Ah," he says, "ah."

"Why shouldn't I be angry? You have allowed my gourd to die. And besides I am in agony here. You promised me comfort."

"I promised you deliverance, Jonah, never comfort. There is an important distinction."

"Well, that may be," I say, "that may be," and lean forward to peer through the haze at the upright city of Nineveh, the dwellings and the marketplace in the distance, all signs of community still there, "but nonetheless I want to know when you are going to get rid of these people. You made me prophesy their doom at considerable risk and I can see very distinctly that the city is still standing. I don't think that's fair."

"Fair?" he says, "What is fair?"

"It is that question to which you people are going to be addressing yourself through eternity," he says, "don't look for any quick answers here."

"You have humiliated me," I say weakly. "I have no time for your sophistry now."

"You have time for anything I say you must, Jonah. Remember who is controlling this."

"How could I forget?" I say. The disputation is endless. On and on it will go through the millennia, this intimate and horrid contact with a figure who is infinitely removed, yet in some strange way equally vulnerable. "How would you let me forget anything? You're always there and you're always insistent."

"So are you, Jonah. So are you."

"But you have all the power."

"If I did," he says sadly, "if I did would I need to thrust you in the body of a whale? Would I need to send you wandering to plead my case for the people? No, I have no power; all that I have is the means to destroy, not to shift and that is no power at all, don't you see? Jonah, you take pity on the gourd which was born in a night and died in a night—"

"Now wait a moment," I say, "wait a moment, it isn't the *gourd* on which I take pity so much as *myself,* the gourd was just a means of protection—"

"Let me finish," he says imperiously, "be quiet." He pauses as if to reclaim his line of reasoning. "You take pity on that gourd; why should *I* not take pity upon forty thousand people who cannot discern their right hand from their left and also much cattle?''

The question rings in the desert and inside me; I ponder it at some length. It is worth consideration but I am not a sophisticated man; there is no other way to put this. I am accustomed to activity, circumstance, outcome which is one of the reasons why I have found working for him so very difficult. "Hair-splitting," I grumble at last, "mere sophistry. That isn't the issue at all."

"It isn't? What is the issue?"

"Keeping promises," I say, "that's what it is. Could you perhaps manifest me a little water to sip? I'm desperately thirsty; I can barely speak—"

"Forget the water, right now. Whose promises aren't being kept? Mine? Or yours?"

"Both of ours of course."

"I made no promises to them. You did."

"Only at your behest."

"*You* went in front of them and promised destruction, not me, so you're embarrassed that I won't follow through. You aren't concerned for me at all, Jonah, you're concerned for yourself."

"I wouldn't even have done this except for you," I say desperately. "Who was I, what was I? A peaceable man living to myself, I made no promises, no commitments, I didn't care what was going on. I had never *heard* of Nineveh before you started all of this with me, what did I give a damn if a bunch of people somewhere to the west were being unjust? I just wanted to live my simple life but you plucked me out of all that, filled me with terrible words and threats, taught me about inequity and injustice and you finally got me involved in all of this, don't you see? You got me as crazy as you, you tossed me into the whale, sent me here, whispered all kinds of things about the Ninevites . . . you can't change everything at the last moment on a *whim,* turn this on me when you started the whole thing—"

"Jonah," he says, "Jonah, I do not like your reply. It is unsatisfactory. I cannot accept it." He begins to laugh insanely, such laughter as I have never heard, rings and peals and bells of torment and smites me wildly upon the head, cracking circumstance further, clapping me to the ground, squeezing me with terrific force against the sands and I find myself afflicted (and not for the first time and surely not for the last I now know) with perception of the absolute perversity of this creature who dwelleth within me. Who dwelleth within me at all times. Who dwelleth within me yet. There is no end to it.

"And don't forget the cattle," he says in a screaming cackle before all the lights fail and I am carried away from there. "Don't ever forget the cattle."

I envisioned a benign and knowledgeable life. Who was to know? Everything at eighteen seems clear; the patterns are crystalline. Wandering through the chutes at play I saw them dragging an old man to the exit trap. Their gear was on, their revolvers poking him along. The old man stared at me. "Don't believe a word of it!" he screamed. "Nothing's changed! They're still liars, assassins, the only difference is that they've learned to do it in the dark." One of them slammed him on the head and he fell heavily, bleeding, the others gathered him in and hoisted. Then they turned on me. "I don't know anything," I said and raised my hands in a posture of prayer. "I don't know anything at all," and they seemed to ponder me for a long time, then they shrugged and walked away. If they had had more definite program, I later ascertained, they would have carried me away as well but they were not prepared at that early stage for intervention. Later on, of course, they learned they should have. Ruth, my third affectional had lost her father to the conveyors before I knew her, she insisted that something was wrong with the apparatus of the state. "It is not as you think," she whispered to me once, "they say they have changed, that they are benign, that the revolution accomplished its ends but this is simply not so, you cannot trust them, you cannot trust any of them," but when I attempted further information, when I tried to find out what she meant she froze and would not speak and one day was no more; her cubicle was emptied, her number removed from the postings and those few of us who knew her were advised that she had left for the Southern Complex. There was that. In the times before Edna there were small shocks, larger hints, but the greater ax of the state did not come upon me as it did not come upon most of us; I was able to live my life outside consequence but it would have had to end. What occurred to me only when I was too deep in the hypnotics to possibly leave, too embraced in their clasp was that the program had been created, perhaps, for people exactly like me: it would filter out the prophets and malcontents, fanatics and dreamers, those whose insights would lead them inevitably to opposition if they could not be drained off by the dream clinics. I saw it, I saw it but by then it was too late; it was only the dream clinic which I wanted. It must have been that way or why was I here?

"That's right," Edna says softly, "that's right, Harold; now you know what has happened to you." Her voice pulses in the blood. "Keep on, keep on, that is the way to the truth."

I lunge against the straps in fury. "Bitch!" I say, "Liar!" and scream in fury understanding the insidiousness of their plan, how they are working to get at me but it will not do, it will not do, "You can't do this to me!" I scream, "I am strong, I know the truth, I am in control!" and all dwindles, the image of the old man in the conveyors as well, all of it vanity, folly and vanity saith the preacher and they will not get me they will not get me they will not get me yet. In this time. In this season.

The thieves, unfortunately, are dead, but I, sterner material indeed am still alive to the pain of the sun when I feel those nails slide free. I plunge a hundred feet into the arms of the soldiers. They cushion my fall, lave my body with strong liquids, murmur and murmur until slowly I crawl over the sill of consciousness. I stare at them. Their faces are entirely sympathetic; I would not have thought there was so much compassion in them. One of them leans over me. He looks familiar but I cannot quite place him. Perhaps he is one of those who stood by Pilate. There have been so many faces in my short life; it is hard to sort them out. His eyes are blank but forgiving.

"Forgiving eyes," I say, "forgive them."

"Forgive who?"

"Forgive them all for they know not what they do."

"Oh, no. You're quite wrong there as usual. You've been wrong all along, I'm sorry to say. They know *exactly* what they do, chief, and so do you."

"Never," I say, "never, never, never, never."

"It won't end that easily," he says, "you'd better accept that for a fact."

"Then crucify me."

"You're not going to be crucified. That's precisely the point. Did you think that that was the way out?"

"Didn't you?"

"No, we did not. We understand what you will come to understand; that you just have to live it, partake of it, take it inch by inch through all the hours and corridors of circumstances and that there are no fires, no celebrations for us but only this certitude and burden right straight through to the end."

"Then make it the end. Make it the end now."

"No such luck. You see, that is not a matter of our choosing. We must live as if it were eternal. And in that assumption, to be sure, we make it so."

"Then this must be hell," I say, weakly but with anger. "This must be hell and I still in it."

"Yes," he says, "oh yes."

He slaps me across the face, a dull blow with much resonance. The brain, turgid, yelps with surprise. "No," I say, "yes. Never. Always. Possible. Impossible." He slaps me again. I spit blood. "I will not yield," I say, "I will not yield; this is not right and yours is not the answer."

"You're not being reasonable," he says, "it is enormously frustrating, I must admit that. You're giving us terrible problems, Harold. We've never dealt with any of them who held on as long as you. And for what point? What purpose? That is what we are unable to deduce. What are you holding on *for?*"

"That is my concern. My option, my decision, don't you think?" I say. Blood fills my cheeks, I expectorate. "That's none of your business."

"I'm afraid it is."

"Help me up there again," I say, "put me up on that fucking cross. It is not sufficient until it is done and if it were to be done it must be. Put me up there, you son of a bitch, hammer the nails in and do it right. There's no other way that you'll ever get me."

"Obsessive. Crazy."

"Hang me on that cross and let it be done."

"Oh Harold, Harold," the hard and terrible man says, "Harold this is impossible, will you stop it, will you simply admit that it can't be carried on further?"

"Jamais," I say, "never."

"Then it will go on and on."

"That's how you warned me it would be though,

wasn't it? Inch by inch and hour by hour. Until the end which we cannot reckon because it is beyond our control."

"You infuriate."

"I understand testimony," I say, "I understand truth. I accept my condition and sooner or later you must come to accept yours as the state must too."

"God damn it—"

"Don't curse," I say admonishingly, "you are in the presence of the Christ here." And close my eyes thoughtfully to wait for ascent and the perfect striation, the known stripes, the nails through the wrist, vaulting, stigmata, pleasure, ascension. Pain.

And other conditions.

"Aren't you tired of this?" the serpent says, "haven't you had enough of it, already? Why don't you simply give up? It could go so much easier."

"I've had enough of dialectic," I say, "enough of disputation; why don't *you* accept the truth, that our battle will continue through eternity and that there will be no end of it?"

"But *you* created it! I'm an aspect of your mind. You can imagine me out of existence as quickly as you willed me into it. You didn't have to have things this way; it was your decision."

"The climactic struggle," I say, "you're looking for it, you dream of it. Except that it cannot be that simple; it will be carried on and on—"

"Your decision," the serpent says, "always your decision, the way you wanted it. Nod, the Garden, Nineveh, Judas, the Book of Revelations. For every one of your creations its opposite; for every benificence an act of darkness." He flicks his tongue, squirms to a higher branch. "Well," he says, "have it your way. It's your decision. Just don't complain to me about it. Don't say that I'm responsible when all along it's your show." He yawns, revealing a fetching tongue, much thicker than I would have conceived and delicately constructed; he flicks it out and catches a leaf dangling from a near branch, brings it back, chews on it. "Comfort me with apples," he murmurs, "but in their absence I'll be glad to have a branch. You take what you can get."

"You really think that I'm responsible for all of this?" I say. His conundrum, although I have heard it before, has finally intrigued me. "That I created this?"

"Of course. You created everything."

"Granted that this is so—which I don't accept for an instant but granting it for the purpose of argument—why would I do it? What could the reason possibly be?"

"Don't ask me," the serpent says, swallowing convulsively and leaning out for another leaf, "that's not what I'm qualified to say at all. I guess you're inalterably perverse but how would I know? I don't know anything more than you."

"It doesn't make sense. It just doesn't make sense that I would create all of this chaos. I never wanted it to be this way; it just evolved—"

"It amuses you," the serpent says, "for all I know you obtain a constant sense of vindication. Maybe you were bored with the void and merely wanted some activity. How would I know? You expect too much. You always were demanding, you know."

"Not really. I was reasonable—"

"Be it as you will. You were reasonable. I don't care." The serpent chews the second leaf quickly, methodically, curls his tail around and composes himself for sleep. "I've got very little more to say," he says, "wake me when the gate of Revelation swings open and I'll see what I can do. I mean, I'm willing to fulfill my role here but I'm not interested in consultation; you'll have to seek other sources for that." He closes his enormous, limpid eyes. "I'd just try to face the truth," he says.

His breath pours out evenly; he does indeed seem to have entered upon a state of sleep. Alone once again in the iron and limitless void I think of what he has said, think of all of his perversities and his taunts and conclude that it is impossible, he can be given no credence whatsoever, disputation is his special province and he would be able to twist it to serve his own purpose but he cannot be believed: how could he be believed? If he were telling the truth then all of this would be nonsense, self-willed trash and of no significance whatsoever. And that simply cannot be because otherwise there would not have been so much pain in it nor justification for the pain.

So I lash out at him in rage and kick him off the branch, send him tumbling in sleep the thousands of eons below where he will nest and alone in the heavens I roar and I roar as the black and luminous curtain of circumstance begins once again its rise. Knowing that this will be for the last time is sufficient for my purposes and like a needful and wide-eyed child I perch before the stage of event, waiting to see what next must happen.

That face, the face looking at me is Edna's but this is strange. I cannot understand it because Edna will not, of course, be born for many centuries but what makes it even stranger is the fact that despite this I recognize her. How can this be? How can I recognize the unborn? This was certainly not part of the prophesy; it imparts a species of presence which is not so mystical as occult. My miracles were never trashy, they were smooth and functional, calculated to the moment with the best of taste and I have always been contemptuous of those who would, say, have yielded caviar and duck rather than loaves and fishes, made the Magdalene a saint when it was sufficient to make her human . . . but it has been imputed to me that I can deduce the identity of the unborn and nothing to do but accept it. At this late stage I accept everything; there is no alternative.

One simply must learn to put up with dislocations and small shocks if one is to be a martyr; it allows one to deal with the larger shocks ahead. Go with the circumstance. If it is Edna and I recognize her, then let that be sufficient. "Hello, Edna," I say. I raise a hand in greeting. It is overcome with lassitude, I am still suffering the effects of crucifixion but I am unfailingly courteous. "How are you? Why are you here?"

She leans close to me, a pretty distressed woman

of the kind who observed the troops casting lots over the vestments, decent enough to be concerned but certainly not courageous enough to intervene. The world operates through the limited decency of women such as this just as it will have to make do on modest miracles. "They said you would recognize me," she says, "I didn't think so but that was their promise. I should have believed them; I should have believed everything they said, if I had I'd be better off now."

"I don't know what you're talking about. Je fail comprende, mon Edna."

She lets a look of sheer disgust flood into her eyes. "You don't know what I'm talking about? I don't know why I'm here. I didn't want to be; I told them it would be of no use whatsoever. But I'm here and I'll talk to you."

"About what?"

"I'll tell you what they said I should! Will you let me speak?" She claws at her face. "This is really too much," she says, "Harold, I should never have been involved in any of this, I never bargained for it, it isn't fair—"

I stare at her. "I am Jesus," I say. "Who is Harold? Call me by my proper name."

"Harold, you've got to stop this nonsense! Now, do you hear me? Everybody's disgusted and a little frightened and it has to come to an end. Stop it!"

"Do you want it to stop?" I say mildly, "Then you could begin to help by getting me out of here." I pluck at my clothing which is quite dirty and showing the effects of several days being the subject of cast lots as well as being the apparel at

Passover. "My appearance is disgusting, frankly, and it's hardly possible to have any self-respect when I look like this. Or when I'm confined to a place like this."

"It's hopeless," she says, "I can see it now. The whole thing is hopeless."

"You won't talk to them about my being released? Then you could have the decency to tell them to hurry up and order a crucifixion. It didn't *quite* take the first time but that's no reason not to try again. I'm in a dehabilitated condition and it won't take long and that will bring an end to this to be sure. Frankly, I'd rather not be crucified again, it's just plain painful Edna, if you want to know, nothing exalting about it at all, but if the decision is to have it done then I think it should be. The important thing is to get me out of here because this is absolutely futile. There's no possibility for an ascension until I'm finished in this place, don't you see? I can't rise before I entirely fall. And I haven't entirely fallen yet; that should be clear to you. It's embarrassing."

"I'm embarrassed," she says. She runs a hand over her cheek. In this posture she looks somewhat like Mary which would be an interesting speculation except that I am in too much pain now to be of a metaphysical turn of mind. If she were Mary in another guise it would compose an interesting diabolism; worthy of the serpent himself. "I'm embarrassed for you, for both of us, for all of us being involved in this situation. They think that I can reason with you but I know that's impossible; I keep on telling them that, I say it's ridiculous, he's too far gone, I know Harold and once he's over the edge on something he's over the edge but they say to try so I'm here doing that. I think that they're as stupid as you and that's the truth Harold, they're just the same as you are, they're trying to make this work. All of you are stupid, the whole bunch, you've let this terrible process take over and you don't even understand it. Face reality, Harold, will you? Harold, you've got to face it and get out of this or it's going to be very bad for me too; they hold me *responsible*, don't you see? They seem to think that I've had something to do with this and I can't change their minds, I can't make them—"

"Jesu," I remind her. "The kingdom and the power and the glory. Forever. And ever. Amen. Amen."

She turns away from me. "Do you see?" I hear her say. "It's absolutely hopeless. Tell me I can stop this."

"Persist," a voice says, "you've barely started."

"It's *humiliating*. How can I stand here like a fool, talking to a crazy man—"

"Persist," the voice says flatly. "You have not even tried yet. The stakes are high. The issues are considerable."

"Nothing can come of this. He's lost to me, to all of us. I told you that it was a waste—"

"What is a waste?" I ask curiously, "you're telling me that I went through all of this for nothing? I don't believe it. I refuse to accept that."

"See?" the voice says, "he's in contact. You can't give up when you haven't even tried. That wouldn't be right at all. Go on. Go on now."

She turns back toward me. Flushed by the dialogue, the aspect of her face is sharp; her eyes glow fluorescent in the intensity. "Listen to me, Harold," she says.

"Jesus."

"You are *not* Jesus or anyone else of your religious figures. You are simply yourself, this is 2219 and you have been undergoing an administered hypnotic procedure."

"They warned me about the tempters," I say, "the tempters and the Comforters."

"You've been living through your religious *obsessions*," Edna says, "but you've been one of those rare cases where you've failed to come back fully into contact, at least that is the way they put it to me, and now you're in blocked transition or something like that. They're trying to help you, they're working on reversing the chemotherapeutic process or whatever it's called but in order to begin you have to accept the facts."

"What facts?" I say. Mild reasonableness fills me; I am anxious to allay her concern. There is no question but that this woman cares for me or at least is attempting to simulate care. "The facts are devastating and I have accepted them. Can't you tell that? Who would submit to Calvary, to crucifixion unless he was entirely trusting? You misunderstand."

"*You* misunderstand. Oh, god damn it, Harold, they're trying to *help* you. That isn't too much, is it? I mean, that isn't too much for you to accept, that you're in this situation and that they're trying to make things better for you. If you make that one little concession they tell me that all the other things will fall into place and you'll have your life back."

"Edna," I say, "my life was an agony. I couldn't wait for them to put me up on that cross. The cross of fire was the only way out and you better believe it."

"Was it? Was it really?"

"I don't want to go back to the passion. It was intolerable; it was redeemed only by the crucifixion. Without it, it would have been a disgraceful life, mean and empty and without purpose of any sort."

"Your life was not the passion, Harold."

"Oh yes it was," I say, "yes it was."

She turns away again. "Do you see?" I hear her say, "it's impossible. Will you let me go now?"

"He is in deep withdrawal," the voice says, "that is inarguable."

"You did it to him."

"Not at all. These cases are inevitable statistically; a certain small proportion will react in this fashion. There is no culpability."

"I could hate you for this," I hear her say, "but I won't. All that I want you to do is to let me alone."

"Leave her alone," I say to the voice, "it isn't her fault. Destiny is resolute. If you are without sin, cast the first stone. Before this day is out I will dwell with her in Heaven."

"I can't deal with it," I hear Edna say, "I can't deal with it; there's no way that you should make me—"

"I want to rise," I say. "It is almost time for the ascension. The night is almost out. Where are my robes, my disciples? Where are the sacred scrolls and the voice of the Father? I'm in a hurry now and this can't go on indefinitely. Bring me the sacred texts; take me to the mountain. If you don't cooperate you will be dealt with very harshly, I assure you."

"Harold," Edna says, "Harold, I'm giving up, I'm going away now. There are no sacred scrolls or followers, there's nothing like that at all. Those people of whom you are speaking died a long time ago."

"So did I," I say indisputably, "but it's time for me to rise again."

"This is your last chance," she says, "and you'd better take it. Who knows what the alternative might be? Who knows what these people might be capable of doing if you don't straighten out? They destroy their mistakes, you know that, you know how the century works now. They trapdoor the decompensates and take them off to the slaughter bins. *We've seen it.*"

"Magdalene," I say reasonably, "the fact that you are a whore does not mean that you speak only truth. I would not sentimentalize your profession as so many others do."

"Harold—"

"It's time, harlot, for you to accept the conditions which brought you here and work with them. You cannot live in a sentimental fallacy all of your life."

"Bastard," she says. Her face congests. She spits.

I leave the spittle there. It is proper. The damp glows on my face, shades toward burning. It is a celebration. A stone. A stigmata.

A cross of fire.

"I never denied you," Job says. "Now it's time for you to make good on your promise." He is weeping, exhausted, but within him glows a hard purpose. "Fair is fair."

"There were no commitments at all," I say. "No promises."

"There was an implied promise," he says, "that if I kept faith you would restore me to my condition." The Comforters nod in agreement. "All along that was understood."

"I'm sorry," I say, "you misunderstand the situation. No promises, no commitments. No restoration."

"You're trying to tell him that he went through all of this for nothing?" one of the Comforters said.

"He went through all of it for his own sake."

"Address the question."

"You can't bully me," I say, "I am the Lord, thy God—"

Job stands and looks at me, his face filled with hatred. "Don't give me that," he said, "don't try to pull rank on me. It doesn't mean a goddamned thing and you know it. If you were omnipotent you wouldn't have let this happen to me!"

"Why not?" I say, "Why not?"

The question is devastating. Even the Comforters look amused. "See," one of them says, "I told you—"

"But that's impossible!" Job says, "That's impossible, that you would permit—"

"You misapprehend the Testaments, then," I say, "you misapprehend the sense of them all," and the dialogue is finished, there is really nothing more to say, I distance myself from them in that special and mystical fashion which has always characterized my dialogues. At a far distance, a great remove I watch what they do then, they talk with one another in consternation, strike at one another, begin to move in empty, purposeless little circles. Job kicks at one of the Comforters and misses, falls to the ground gripping his foot, bellows with pain, rocks back and forth. The Comforters point at them and then they walk through the gates and into the fields. On his knees Job bellows and shakes his fist at them but they do not turn back.

Regretfully I consider the situation and decide against joining him once more. It would change nothing; it would merely be to drive the hard insight over again, the polished and final statement. He knows now. All of them know.

They misunderstood. There was never anything that I could do at all. I did not want to.

Satan was merely the excuse.

Conveyed rapidly toward Calvary I get a quick glimpse of the sun which appears in strobes of light as they drive me with heavy kicks toward the goal. A brutal bunch, uneducated, unaware of the seriousness of the issues; to them I am merely another felon being set on course. For all I know, Pilate felt the same and was merely humoring me. All of them humoring me. Nonetheless, my yoke is easy at this time and the burden light, I have fed my flock and it is a speedy journey that I will make from the court to this place although not as easy as the one that I will make, soon enough, to my Father's side. I know how it will be: a few strokes of the hammer, some pain at the outset: blood, unconsciousness, the grateful and graceful ascension. Nothing will be easier than that, I think. Crucifixion is nothing; it is the arriving at this condition which has made all the difficulty. Crucifixion will be a pleasure. Struggling with the sacred texts has been boring, the miracles sheer utility, the wrestling matches absorbing but purposeless, the disciples a seedy and naive bunch. There have been no relationships of value, everything has been locked to the context of performing a single mission, arriving at this end.

Regarding everything that I have been through in this tumultuous year I can see that it has come to nothing, that even the most celebrated moments have occurred outside of me and that the inner decay, the weariness, the uselessness of what I have been doing has permeated my condition. Disciples, beggars, moneychangers, penitents, harlots, peasants and thieves, the stone-littered roads, the desert, the straggling camps at the edge of the cities, the troops, the diseased horses . . . only in the testaments has this period achieved any aura; it must surely qualify as one of the most impoverished and purposeless in the history of civilization. At its fringes I have conducted my business, a wanderer amidst wanderers, itinerant prophet to the masses, fanatic among many fanatics and there has been almost nothing to distinguish me from the rest of them; the miracles have been genuine but for all I know so have the other rumored miracles; in gossip everything becomes the same and the greatest of passions becomes only the credibility problem of the provinces. It has been a wasting, testing time, impossible to view in any context other than fatigue and if it were not for the end which has been decreed it had no meaning whatsoever. I must accept this; only the passion and the Crucifixion are able to imbue this with meaning.

But I will not be the only itinerant crucified; many of the wanderers and fanatics have wound up hammered for the masses. While my condition may be unique my outcome is not; crucifixion was one of the most popular means of execution in this time bereft of technology: in later eras they learned to do it by fire, flood, the ovens or great incendiary devices whereas here they had to make do with a cross and a few large nails; it is a painful way in which to die but not a particular. There have been no particulars in this all along; at no point could I aspire to uniqueness and that is, perhaps, the ultimate of the deception which has been visited upon me. I was not a special case at all, not to the times, even to myself.

"Faster!" they scream to me, "Faster!" Their shouts break this futile internalization and almost gratefully I lengthen my stride to their urging. The cross is bound to my wrist, bears upon the slope of my back but my legs are free and I am able to run, the cross driving me into the ground at every step. "Faster!" they scream, "Carry it, carry it!" and in the dark of my throat I say *yes, faster, faster* and struggle to push that burden. Vite, vite, vite mon freres to that great mountain where I will show them at last and beyond any dispute that passion has as legitimate a place in this world as any of their policies and procedures and that it will last: I will convince them as I have already tried to convince myself, a hell of a lot longer. Brava passione!

Brava crucifixus! Because if this at least will not last, if it is not the truth and if the crucifixion will not survive the centuries then I have been lied to on levels so profound that I will be unable to deal with them, then my life, all of it, will have been a lie and nowhere to go, nowhere to go. It must survive the centuries, it must go on and on and yet as the cross begins to bind, as my legs flutter, as the terrible heaving of the chest overtakes, warning that the heart itself may be beginning to go, as all of this happens I come to understand that there is a very good likelihood that it *does* mean nothing but that that does not excuse me for a moment from the commitment to act as if it did. And as it must. And as it would.

Brava passione!
Brava!

Nailed on the cross that is Edna I gather to thunder into her. My arms and legs hunch, my breathing constricts, I clutch in the motions of generation and slowly unfurl to her a silken thread on which I move, on which I scream. "Yes, now!" she shrieks and impaled upon her I am fixed to that instant of fire which pins me forever, that great screaming bird of fire on the high mountain in the time that is not Biblical, on the mountain which is not Calvary.

So finally, finally now they yank me from the restraints and toss me into the center of the huge room so that I can meet the actors. The production is over, they insist, this is the only way that it can reach terminus. There they are, there all of them are: congregants, disciples, Romans, pagans, troopers, serpent, Job, Magdalene, other of my friends and all of the paraphernalia and armament of my mission. Edna alone is missing, they must have responded to her insistence, at least she would have been there if she could have borne it. I must take that on faith. I must take everything on faith; in the end it has destroyed me but I know nothing other and there is more credibility in faith—is there not?—than in its lack.

"Enough," Pilate says. He comes toward me, rubbing his hands briskly, little empty patches in his makeup revealing the bald, weary actor underneath. "Enough, Frederick. That's your name, isn't it, Frederick?"

"Harold."

"Good enough," he says, "it's all the same to me, you know, it's just a job, do it here, do it there, strike the set, get onto the next, hard to keep them straight but no offense, young man, none at all. You've done very well, my fellow, quite nicely, but the performance is over, our revels now are ended so to speak and it's time to go onto other things."

"Are you still pleased you gave them Barabbas?"

"Barabbas?" He looks at me in confusion, then comprehension hits him. "Oh," he says, "oh yes, I remember, that business on the steps, of course. Now, that's far behind us."

"But are you happy?"

"It's all a role," Pilate says, "that's all, they give you the script, you go out, do the best you can, go onto the next. Can barely remember this stuff as soon as it's over. Anyway, Frederick, it's time for you to clean all of this out of your mind and get back to your life. You'll be the better for it, you understand."

"I don't know what you're talking about."

"Sometimes you can really get involved, Frederick; it's possible to take this stuff so seriously that it takes a bit longer to come back than it should. But we all must come back sooner or later. Anyway," Pilate says, "that's all *I* have to say. That's what they wanted me to tell you and I did." He inclines his head, steps back. In the rear Simon Peter raises his hand. "It's all done for, Master," he says, "like the loaves and fishes, you understand? When something's eaten, it's eaten. It's consumed, you know what I mean, mate?"

"Absolutely right," Paul says, standing next to him. "So just get hold of yourself, Fred and everything will be fine. You did good, real good."

"My name is *Harold*."

"Sorry, chief," Simon Peter says. "Awful hard to keep those names straight as we said, there are so many of these for us to do. Anyway, Harold, don't worry about a thing."

They look at me, rows and rows of them. Congregants from Bruck Linn are there and the assassins from the mosque; I recognize the troopers who cast lots to say nothing of many in the crowd who shouted for Barabbas. It is a compelling and frightening experience to see all of these specters of recent weeks arrayed against me so; I was not even aware that many of them knew one another but now, indisputably, there they are. This must be one of the aspects of the Tomb; I must be in that stage between the Crucifixion and the Resurrection. I wave at them cheerfully. "Not much longer," I say, "don't worry about a thing; soon enough I'll be risen."

"You're not going to be risen," somebody says, "nothing more is going to happen at all. This is the finish, Harold."

"Ne rien," I say, "this is the beginning."

"You'd just better face it, Harold. We've gone to a lot of trouble to gather for you, to show you what the situation is. Usually, this kind of thing isn't done at all."

"Ne rien," I repeat. I fold my arms. "Not to worry."

The serpent slithers over to me, coils himself at my foot, raises his head, regards me fetchingly from yellow eyes. "You don't believe them," he says, "so will you believe *me?* They're telling you the truth, Harold. It was all a play."

"All a play? You too?"

"Me more than the rest of them. Prince of masks, you know," the serpent says. He licks a foot shyly. "All for the best, Harold. Just wait and see.

Better to go back to your life than to emerge from the Tomb, you know."

"I don't believe it," I say.

"I know you don't believe it, but there it is old chum. The truth, whether you like it or not. We all have to accept the truth at some point or go mad."

"Ne rien," I repeat, "I will not yield. I will not believe what you are saying."

"Oh come on, Harold," the serpent says, "you won't listen to them, at least listen to *me;* I'm your old companion in arms, your tempter, your colleague, your conspirator, your friend. Stop it already. If you don't, it's going to get worse."

"It can't get worse."

"Oh yes it can. Take it from me, leader of all damnation; there is much worse for you ahead, Harold unless you go along with this now. Would I lead you wrong?"

I stare at him, lift my foot, put it on his head. He twists desperately as I begin to apply pressure. I lean on the foot, raise the other, put the weight of my body in him. There is a terrible, diminished shrieking under my foot. I raise it and point at his mangled head. "Do you see?" I say. They stare at me shocked as well they might. "The devil is dead," I say. "I have vanquished Satan. He has bruised my heel but I sure as hell have bruised his head."

I begin to laugh insanely. It is that release to which I am entitled, that release which I have forestalled for so long and at last am allowed to pour forth. I do so luxuriantly. There is a sensation of passage, benediction. "I told you that it would be this way!" I say between little bursts and peals, "I told you that the prophecy would be fulfilled! Swine! Fools!"

A great clout strikes.

Something knocks me to the floor. I feel the hard, gleaming surface rush, strike me and propel me to the lip of consciousness. It hurts. Nothing, not even the nails, not even the wrestling in the desert hurt me so much. But I could have expected nothing less; I knew that it would have to end this way. If I was spared nothing throughout, would I be spared at the end? Would I? I scramble for purchase, somehow manage to hurl myself upright. I will meet them standing. They will not put me down. Attende bien: they will not put me down. My capacity to absorb pain is almost limitless, that they should have known if they had observed the activities of this time.

"I will not yield," I say flatly. "Do you hear me? You can seduce, enchant, but nothing will change; I will always be the same. I have slain the serpent: do you think that I would perish under the blows of fools?"

Pilate steps forward. His eyes are intense yet not without a certain sympathy. "Listen," he says, "we've tried everything here and it can't go on."

"Then release me."

"We can respect what you're doing," Pilate says. "Truly, there is much to be said for your obsession, your stubbornness; you have taken a position and you will follow it through and this is admirable. We've never had anyone quite like you, frankly, but it's got to stop because the risks are too great."

"Then stop it," I say, "just stop it. "All of that is within your means."

"It's a complex and risky treatment process," Pilate says nervously. "Expensive and quite controversial; something like this, if you don't pull out of it could raise unanswerable questions, cause it to be suspended and what would happen then? There are all kinds of people who have to be controlled—"

"I don't know what you're talking about," I say, "what treatments, what control? This is apostasy."

He stares at me intently. "I think you're telling the truth," he says, "I believe you at least. I think you're so trapped in this thing that you don't know anymore who you are or what is happening to you or what it means."

"I know who I am," I say, "I know exactly who I am and so do you. Don't you?"

"You're beyond reason, aren't you?" Pilate says. "That's the exact truth, you can no longer be talked to."

I confront him reasonably. I am a reasonable man. If I am nothing else I am that and always will be. "Of course I know who I am," I say, "and I will see you with my Father in heaven."

"Oh my," Pilate says, "oh my, oh my, oh my—"

"Of course that's where I will see you and not a bloody moment sooner than that. I deny you now. I deny all of you and I will deal with you no more."

I try to turn but he puts a hand on my shoulder, wrenches me around, thrusts his face at me. "You have got to understand what you're doing," he

163

says, "you must. The penalties can be enormous; they involve all of us, the entire state, the system itself rides on your circumstance. It's got to be controlled, this is the way to control it, otherwise—"

"Otherwise," I say, "you will lose your world."

"That is exactly right," Pilate says. The others murmur. "I have gotten through to you, then. That is right. We will lose our world. All of us. You too."

"It is well *worth* losing," I say. "I have considered this, I have given it a great deal of thought. I did not permit myself casually to go into the desert nor accept the terrible burdens that were placed upon me; I am a thoughtful man, I know of stakes and consequence. Martyrdom is not a posture, not at all."

Someone applauds, stops quickly.

"Martyrdom springs from the heart," I continue, encouraged. "I am absolutely serious, it did not begin that way as we know but that is the fashion in which it has ended. And O Lord I will not yield, I will not apologize, I will not be moved."

His hand falls from me, he shakes his head. "You are a fool," Pilate says, "you are a fool on behalf of all of us and we will pay a price that you can never know."

"I will not be moved," I say again. "Thy will be done, pater noster and besides, once you get going on this stuff you can't just turn it off. It was meant to be taken seriously, it can really get hold of you, don't you know that?"

"Oh yes," Pilate says, "oh yes, oh yes. I know that to be sure. It can really get hold of you."

"It's got hold of me," I say, "and I believe it. I believe every word of it and I always will. Tear the stone open and carry me from the Tomb; I will be on my way from here, forever."

"Are you sure you know what you mean?"

"I know exactly what I mean. I couldn't be more sure; I couldn't have less doubt."

Pilate looks at me sadly. His eyes convey infinite knowledge, infinite remorse. "I think that you're telling the truth," he says, "the others may not believe you but *I* do. I think you really mean it this time."

"With all my heart," I say.

"So be it," Pilate says, "so be it."

He makes a motion and the others shuffle close to me. Simon Peter tries to catch my way across all this distance but I ignore him. I ignore them all. "Harold," the Magdalene cries from the back, "Harold, you don't know—"

"Yes I do."

"There's still time; right up to the last moment, right up to the end of it, Harold, you can change—"

"No," I say. "I cannot. It was foreordained." This is the absolute truth. "There was never any possibility for change at all once this began."

"He's right," Pilate says, "on his own terms, in his own right, he is speaking the truth. That must be respected."

There seems to be nothing more to say. Almost embarrassed, they close in upon me. There is less vengeance in their aspect than tentativeness. Than shame. Burning, burning, their countenances catch the shimmer from the walls.

"So be it," Pilate says again. "If that is what he wants, then that is what he must get."

There is a sound of engines. The room shakes as the whine accelerates; underneath a dimmer rumbling. The walls shake, then begin to expand. Little chinks of light pour through the sudden openings; the eyelets appear all over the facade of the temple. They are very close upon me now. I feel their breath.

It would have had to be this way. There is a satisfaction in accepting the utter truth. There is no distance and soon we will be blended. Knowing what they have in mind I am nonetheless relieved. This has gone on too long. Too long.

Too long and no hope for it. "I will not yield," I say to them quietly. This too is what they must hear; at the end I seek to meet all of their pleasures. "I will never yield. I will not apologize. I will not be moved. This isn't folklore, you know, the easy music of the texts. This is real pain. Actual history. The crucialities of martyrdom."

"You ain't kidding," jesting Pilate says.

They move on me.

They tear me apart. Or seek to.

And consequently I move on them. No one ever said that martyrdom had to be passive; I am celebrated for the vigorousness of my action, the determination of my will. I leap into their midst, knock Pilate sprawling, force my way through the assassins at the mosque and head toward the Magdalene. It must be the serpent who gives me this power; I can feel his blood upon my foot, still warm, flooding my own blood, inspiriting. I seize the Magdalene by the arm, drag her toward the corner, shocked they are unable to protect against this. She wriggles against me hopelessly. "Harold," she says, "Harold—" I hold her tightly. She wriggles on my wrist. "Leave me alone," I say to them then, "Leave me alone or I'll kill her."

They stare at me, hesitant for a moment. "I mean it," I say, "the Testaments be damned, one has to protect oneself in situations of this sort. Always."

Then Pilate laughs again. "Fool," he says, "why do you think *that* would stop us? That is exactly what we want."

They advance upon me once more and this time I understand there will be no cessation. I clutch the Magdalene. Sink a thousand years into the deeper pit.

Sinking, I think of Satan once again and am glad that we were able to have not only our struggles but our conversations in the desert, that we had the chance to really get to know one another. To establish a relationship. He was quite right, of course, that old best-loved angel, I can see that now and I wish that I had had the grace to acknowledge it at the time. I wanted him, I wanted him, I called him into this. It was better to have him outside than in that split and riven part of myself. What a fool I was, weak in my capacity, to split off the world trying to dislodge my own pain. It cannot work. Self-delusion of that kind can never work. Look at what they have done to me now. Look at it, consider.

Consider what I have done to myself now.

They do not ignore the limbs nor the more shocking parts.

They leave me on the Cross of fire for forty days and forty nights but on the forty-first the jackals from the south finally gnaw the wood to ash and it collapses.

Unconscious I am carried off, what is left of me in the jaws of the jackals and onto even greater adventures which I dare not in this context mention in all of the bowels and partitions of the divided Earth.

Edna.

Oh, Edna.

1981: New Jersey

WHY WASTE YOUR PRECIOUS PENNIES ON GAS OR YOUR VALUABLE TIME ON LINE AT THE BOOKSTORE?

We will send you, FREE, our 28 page catalogue, filled with a wide range of Ace Science Fiction paperback titles—we've got something for every reader's pleasure.

Here's your chance to add to your personal library, with all the convenience of shopping by mail. There's no need to be without a book to enjoy—request your *free* catalogue today.

CONAN